Beth's heart beat like a bass drum in her ears, and she felt a shiver race up her spine as the front door slammed. There were footsteps on the stairs. And then Jack stood in the doorway . . .

He stepped into the room and closed the door behind him. Slowly he came within touching distance of her. "I remembered why I'd been looking forward to seeing you today. I've thought about it all week. I dreamed about it at night." The glint in his eye foretold his intentions, and she slowly backed away from him. "You have the sweetest mouth I've ever tasted."

Her last step brought her flat against the wall, and Jack was just inches away. "Don't be afraid, Beth. I won't ever hurt you," he murmured, lowering his mouth to hers. The kiss she was expecting to be hard and possessive was soft, gentle, shattering her defenses completely. He knew her anxieties and understood her fears—and his next kiss was aimed at overriding them all. He cradled her in his arms and kissed her throat, her cheeks, her mouth. His touch rippled through her like a tidal wave, washing away layer after layer of painful memory, until there was nothing but Jack and the way he made her feel. . . .

WHAT ARE *LOVESWEPT* ROMANCES?

They are stories of true romance and touching emotion. We believe those two very important ingredients are constants in our highly sensual and very believable stories in the *LOVESWEPT* line. Our goal is to give you, the reader, stories of consistently high quality that may sometimes make you laugh, sometimes make you cry, but are always fresh and creative and contain many delightful surprises within their pages.

Most romance fans read an enormous number of books. Those they truly love, they keep. Others may be traded with friends and soon forgotten. We hope that each *LOVESWEPT* romance will be a treasure—a "keeper." We will always try to publish

LOVE STORIES YOU'LL NEVER FORGET
BY AUTHORS YOU'LL ALWAYS REMEMBER

The Editors

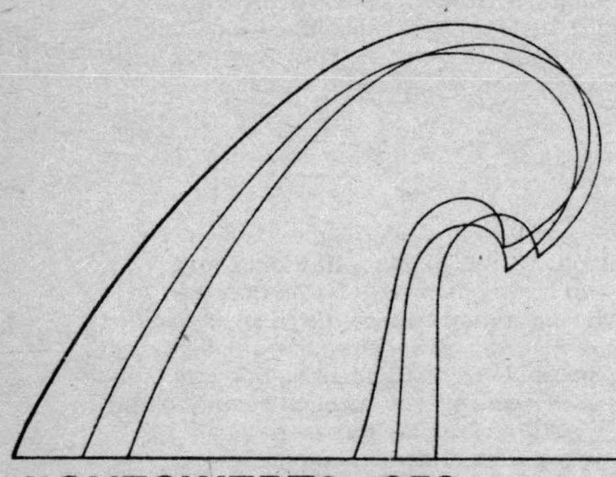

LOVESWEPT® • 358

Mary Kay McComas

Familiar Words

BANTAM BOOKS
NEW YORK • TORONTO • LONDON • SYDNEY • AUCKLAND

FAMILIAR WORDS

A Bantam Book / October 1989

ISBN 0-553-22032-2

Published simultaneously in the United States and Canada

Bantam Books are published by Bantam Books, a division of Bantam Doubleday Dell Publishing Group, Inc. Its trademark, consisting of the words "Bantam Books" and the portrayal of a rooster, is Registered in U.S. Patent and Trademark Office and in other countries. Marca Registrada. Bantam Books, 666 Fifth Avenue, New York, New York 10103.

PRINTED IN THE UNITED STATES OF AMERICA

O 0 9 8 7 6 5 4 3 2 1

For my sisters, Karen and Amy.
Two sides of the same coin.
So different. So much in common.
I love you.

One

The day's high was a summerlike eighty-two degrees at noon. Sure hope you enjoyed it, folks, because the mercury's dropping. Expect a chilly night in the low forties, and guess what? They're calling for rain again in the morning. Is somebody building an ark out there? Tomorrow's high . . .

Jack Reardan switched off the truck's radio. He was covered head to toe with sawdust, mud, and sweat. He was exhausted and madder than hell. He didn't mind loaning his truck out to employees to run company errands, but there had damned well better be gas in the tank at six o'clock when he wanted to go home. Even his daughter Chelsea knew better than to leave his gas tank empty, he fumed inwardly.

Hearing the weather forecast had deepened his angry scowl. It had been raining off and on—mostly on—for the past eight days. The logging roads farther north were barely passable. Already his crew had had to abandon two trucks that had gotten bogged down in the mud. Logging accidents were frequent enough, he knew. He would be inviting trouble by continuing to operate under dangerous weather conditions. If the rain kept up, he'd have to close down for a while. And no one would be too happy about that.

Jack grimaced and sighed defeatedly when he pulled into Donny Anderson's station and saw cars lined up at the gas pumps five and six in a row. In the small town in northern Idaho, the sight was unusual. Odder still was the fact that the place was crawling with teenagers.

Jack spotted Donny lounging in the chair in his office watching the kids who were buzzing about his domain. They had obviously conned Donny into letting them use his gas station to run a car wash.

Jack pulled around the line of car-wash supporters and parked in front of the office door.

"Donny, I'm proud of you," Jack exclaimed with a grin as he walked through the doorway. "After all these years of fightin' 'em, you've finally joined them."

"Hell, Jack, it wasn't my idea," Donny said defensively as he removed his hat and scratched the back of his neck. "One minute I was talking to this nice little lady, and the next minute the whole place was infested with this bunch of rowdies." He replaced his hat in a frustrated manner. He looked confused, as if he still wasn't sure what had happened to him.

"Don't try to tell me you didn't know all their mothers and fathers and friends and relatives would come in to support the kids and then fill up their tanks while they were here."

Jack's smile took on a sly quality as Donny's large round face grew thoughtful and he turned to reconsider the flurry of activity outside his window. Jack's eyes twinkled with humor for the first time that day as his gaze followed Donny's.

The teenagers had literally "taken over" the gas station. They pumped gas and collected the money. They washed the cars and rinsed them, laughing when they "accidentally" lost control of the hose and a classmate got drenched with water. Then they dried and shined the vehicles while a third group vacuumed the interiors. Actually, Jack thought, even with the horseplay the whole process looked quick, efficient, and very well organized.

A short blond girl attracted Jack's attention when she came around the corner of the station and caught sight of his truck. She threw her hands over her face in exaggerated revulsion, then quickly removed them to speak to one of the boys beside her. The young man relinquished his hose to her, and with the most grotesque look of horror on her face, she and her soap squad of students approached Jack's truck.

In the seconds it took Jack to react, the blonde had already sprayed a good quarter of an inch of mud off the side of the truck. With the diligence of the single-minded, she adjusted the nozzle to full force, moving it back and forth across the logo on the door.

"Good grief," she called out to her soapers. "Will you just look at this mess! We could grow corn in all this dirt."

Jack stood motionless as he watched them. He wasn't really angry, but he was definitely peeved that the young woman hadn't asked his permission to wash his truck. People in this neck of the woods had better manners than that, he thought. Jack's face took on the stern expression he usually saved for when his daughter had committed a minor infraction of his rules, while he tried to ignore the fact that the girl's shorts were very . . . short. Then again, it *was* a little hard *not* to notice legs that were perfectly and provocatively shaped, a tank top that fit snugly. . . .

"Hi. This your truck?" The blonde had finally seen him and was smiling up at him happily, unaware that she was about to be taught a lesson in car-wash etiquette.

Jack nodded. He continued to watch her as she sprayed mud off the truck and moved slowly in his direction. There was something different about her, he noted, not sure exactly what it was.

"You work for Reardan Lumber, then," she stated. She glanced at him briefly, then returned her attention to her task.

Jack nodded again. The girl had lovely eyes. They were large and green . . . or maybe light brown. They tilted slightly upward at the corners and danced delightfully. It was obvious that she was enjoying herself tremendously.

Jack looked down at the boy who was moving along in her path with a bucket of suds and a soapy sponge. He was watching Jack carefully, a playful smirk on his face. Jack was well acquainted with Boodle McKenzie, the oldest son of one of his foremen. He winked at the boy good-naturedly, then turned back to the girl, who was speaking but not looking at him.

"You can tell Mr. Reardan that the high school pep club and football team have just saved him a fortune in gasoline. This truck'll probably get ten or fifteen more miles to the gallon now that it doesn't have to drag all this real estate around with it," she said humorously. "And if he's interested, we could discuss a fleet rate, if the rest of his trucks look like this. I wonder if the governor knows that half of northern Idaho is stuck to the sides of Mr. Reardan's trucks?" she speculated, her grin displaying even white teeth and an enchanting set of dimples.

"I don't know. Why don't you write and ask him?" Jack asked her. He would have liked to let the girl go on charming him, but she really did need this lesson. People just didn't go around washing other people's cars without permission—no matter how good the cause. "While you're at it, ask him if there's a law against washing private vehicles without the owner's consent."

The girl's eyes instantly grew larger.

"Oh dear. I am so sorry," she said. She looked crestfallen and was so repentant that Jack began to smile his forgiveness. She drew the spray away from the truck and aimed it at the pavement. The water ricocheted upward and soaked the legs of Jack's pants and boots before pooling at his feet.

In shock, Jack stood staring at her. He heard Boodle McKenzie choking on his laughter and the girl sputtering her apologies. But Jack wasn't sure if he wanted to blow the lid off his temper or simply give up on what was proving to be a perfectly rotten day, and laugh along with Boodle.

In a great fluster the girl finally managed to turn the hose off, then stood holding it in both hands, mortified by what she'd done. "I . . . I don't know what to say. I'm really very sorry for getting you wet and . . . and for washing your truck without asking. I just assumed that every thing on the lot was fair game. I should have known better. I'm sorry," she said. She shifted her weight uncomfortably. "I'm certainly not setting a very good example, am I?" she said.

"Example for who?" Jack asked.

"For whom," she corrected him in an automatic manner, then she closed her eyes and grimaced at her rudeness. Valiantly, she fought her embarrassment and continued speaking. "I'm not setting a very good example for my students." She indicated the teenagers who were gathering around them rapidly. "I'm one of their teachers. My name is Elizabeth Simms," she said with a heavy, fatalistic sigh.

"I'd heard we had a new teacher at the high school." Jack hoped he didn't look as surprised and relieved as he felt. He hadn't been ogling a teenager but a lovely woman. His instincts hadn't failed him after all.

"Great way to make a first impression, huh?" Her smile was weak and self-derisive.

Jack glanced around at the curious faces in the group. He shrugged and let a half smile form on his lips. "No great harm done. Forget it."

"No. I won't forget it. What I did was stupid and irresponsible. At . . . at least let me buy you a new pair of boots."

Although Elizabeth seemed totally sincere in her wish to make amends, her plea initiated a low rumble of chuckles from the boys and some of the girls. Even Jack had to smile at her naïveté.

"What?" she asked with a bewildered frown as she looked around at her students. "What's so funny?"

"Buying me a new pair of boots wouldn't be nearly as hard on you as it would be on me," Jack told her, his temper easing considerably. "They all know that an old pair of worn boots, even soaked and later dried, are more comfortable than a pair of new work boots. Most of them have seen their fathers resole the same pair over and over again until the leather on top wears out rather than have to break in a new pair."

"Oh," she said, deflated. "Well then, what can I do to set things right?"

Again a snicker rippled through the crowd, but only from the boys this time as their teenage minds began to race. Being one of the few unmarried men in town, Jack was used to this sort of humor. But he could tell the teacher wasn't as her cheeks grew brighter in color. Without batting an eye, Jack said, "You can finish washing my truck and I'll bring in my car to be washed as well—"

"For free." She enthusiastically finished the sentence for him and looked very relieved.

"Nope." Jack shook his head. "That would defeat the purpose of the car wash. You pay the costs for both cars, and we'll call it even," he said, watching her closely.

"It's a deal." She stretched out her hand to seal the bargain. "Thank you, Mr. . . ."

"Reardan. Jack Reardan."

Through pursed lips she blew out a sigh. Their hands failed to meet, hers falling away as she realized her third faux pas in almost as many minutes. "Could we please start all over again?" she asked him beseechingly.

Jack gave in to his laughter. His anger melted away when he saw the forlorn expression on her face.

"Hi," she said, stretching her hand out once again, a friendly smile on her lips. "I'm Beth Simms, the new teacher at the high school."

"Nice to meet you, Ms. Simms," Jack said, taking her hand before she pulled it away. "Jack Reardan. Father of one of your students."

Jack was amazed at how soft and small her hand was as it lay wrapped in his large, callused grasp. He thought it strange that she was a teacher. She was so young-looking and so small.

A tension built between them as they stood watching each other, forming impressions. It was several seconds before Jack took note of the alert faces that were still huddled about them. "You teach English literature, right?"

Beth nodded. "And drama. I have Chelsea in both my classes."

"I know. She wanted me to make a point of meeting you at the open house next week."

A fleeting frown crossed the teacher's face. When she spoke, her words were quick and short. "Well, I'll look forward to seeing you then. But right now we'd better get back to work, or we'll be here all weekend."

He didn't know why, but Jack suddenly felt long and reptilian. All at once the teacher seemed repulsed by him. He almost raised his arm to take a whiff of himself, but didn't want to be that obvious. He was very conscious of how he must look to her, covered with a day's worth of grime from the mill, but for some reason he wasn't ready to see this moment come to an end.

"What are you buying with the proceeds from all this?" Jack had to raise his voice to be heard over the jet spray of water she'd aimed at his truck.

"New football uniforms," she called back without looking at him, totally engrossed in the task. "The parents' booster club is helping with the money, but we need to meet them halfway."

"Where's Chelsea? Do you know? Why isn't she here?" His questions were now addressed more to Boodle McKenzie than to Beth. But it was Beth who answered.

"She volunteered to go to the store for more soap and sponges. After that she's going home. She said you had some extra buckets we could use."

She'd stated her answer without so much as a glance in his direction. He was glad to see that she was responsible enough to know the whereabouts of her students when they were in her charge, even though he hadn't been particularly worried about Chelsea. For the most part, he trusted his daughter to know the rules and what he expected of her. But he found himself wanting Beth to look at him when she spoke to him, whether the subject was as important as Chelsea or as insignificant as football uniforms. He wanted this woman's attention, and he was beginning to wonder why it mattered so much to him.

There was no denying, however, that their conversation was over. She made it abundantly clear to Jack as she increased her efforts to appear busy. She even moved around to the other side of the truck with her hose when she became aware that he had taken up a comfortable stance beside one of the pumps and was watching her with great interest. Jack laughed at her evasive maneuver and sauntered back into the office.

"Ain't she a hummer?" Donny asked with an amazed shake of his head, taking in the condition of Jack's pants and boots. "She wasn't in here five minutes before I was telling her I'd be glad to have them kids use my station for their car wash. Took me a few minutes before I even knew I was hit, let alone by what."

"I'll bet. I thought she was one of the kids for a while there."

"Me too. Me too," Donny agreed, puckering his lips and nodding several times. "I made her show me her driver's license. She's a cute little thing, ain't she?"

Jack shrugged and nodded noncommittally. It wouldn't do to have Donny thinking he was impressed with the new schoolteacher. He was well aware that being the most eligible bachelor in a small town left his social life open to public speculation and scrutiny. When he dated, he dated carefully, so the townspeople wouldn't have him engaged, married, and living happily ever after before the date was over. Not that he'd mind, if he were out with the right woman. But Ms. Right didn't live within a hundred-mile radius. He'd checked.

"I hear she bought the old McKenzie place and the boy there is helping her fix it up," the station owner commented, always eager to pass on any information that came his way.

Jack followed the direction of Donny's gaze and, for once, was glad Donny knew more than he had a right to about someone's private life. "Boodle's helping her?" he asked.

Donny nodded thoughtfully. "I reckon that gives her quite a handful to deal with all at once. What with her job at the school, the house, the baby, and now that lovesick Boodle underfoot all the time."

"She has a baby?" Jack was still amazed that she was a teacher. The fact that she was a mother stunned him for a second.

"Scott is his name. Had him in here the other day when she was asking permission to have this car wash. He's a cute little bugger too. Two years old and feisty as hell."

"That's hard to picture. She doesn't look much older than Chelsea," Jack said. He chuckled softly over the dilemma and then, forgetting his earlier resolve to act casually interested, he said, "I swear, Donny, for a couple seconds out there I was actually torn between patting her on the head and patting her bottom. How old is she anyway? Do you know?"

"She's twenty-seven," a female voice answered from the doorway. Both men turned to face Beth. She made no effort to hide the hurt and disappointment in her eyes—or the anger either. She looked straight at Jack and said, "Your truck is ready."

Embarrassed, Jack immediately followed her out into the early twilight. "Ms. Simms. Wait a second. Please," he called. Ignoring his request, Beth walked around the corner of the station and out of view. When Jack caught up with her, he had to grab her arm and swing her around to face him before he could begin his apology. "Hey. Look, I'm sorry. I didn't know you were there."

"That's not exactly saying you're sorry you said it in the first place, only that you got caught," she said pointedly.

"Well, I am sorry I said it. And I'm sorry you heard me."

"Great," she said, accepting his regrets but refusing to forgive him. She shook loose of his hold and began to walk away again.

"Look, Ms. Simms, this is a small town. You're going to be talked about. If you run around in a snit all the time because someone said something about you, you'll only make it worse," he said to her back, taking note of the fact that her hips and her ponytail swayed in opposite directions when she walked.

"Oh, yeah?" she said as she turned around, her expression pugnacious, her eyes blazing with anger as she retraced her steps, narrowing the distance between them. "Well, I'll have you know, Mr. Jack Reardan, that my age, my son, and my bottom are no concern of yours or anyone else's in this town. And I'd appreciate it if you'd *butt* out of my business and not encourage people to talk about me."

"Listen. You were the one who came butting in first. You're the one who attacked my truck with a garden hose, remember?"

"And that gives you the right to be a meddling, intrusive . . . gossipmonger?" she asked.

"It wasn't that big a deal," he said, matching his tone to hers. "I just asked Donny what he knew about you. To tell you the truth, I'm sorry I bothered."

Her eyes narrowed dangerously. "You're free to leave anytime. Your truck is done, and I've paid the two dollars. I've also paid for your car the way we bargained. Just do me the favor of waiting until after noon tomorrow before you bring it in. Okay?"

"Why?"

"So I won't be here."

Her spitefulness and the idiocy of bickering with someone he had to practically bend over double to meet eye to eye struck Jack as humorous. It was like seeing a bear cowering before a blue jay. And he wasn't about to let this little birdie have the last word. Nor would he be so easily dismissed a second time. He tilted forward at the waist, moving his face closer to hers. So close, he could see that her eyes were gold and green and full of spirit. Keeping his voice as serious as he could, he said, "You sure are cute when you're mad, Ms. Simms."

Beth sputtered momentarily as she glanced around and decided how far to go with her rebuttal. Thankfully, most of the students were well beyond hearing distance. Unfortunately for Beth, the words she needed to cut Jack to ribbons seemed to stick in her throat. In frustration she finally threw up her hands, growled at him, and flounced off.

Jack spoke his thoughts aloud. "Lady, if I had that swing of yours, I'd keep it in my backyard," he added, making not the slightest effort to hide his admiring perusal of her and topping off his statement with a laugh.

"Horrible, impudent man," Beth muttered aloud as she got into her car an hour later. She wrapped her woolen coat around her shoulders because of the dropping temperature, adding maliciously, "I hope he runs out of gas on the way home."

Driving home alone, it was all too easy to recall the sinking feeling she'd had when she'd come out from behind Jack Reardan's truck and found that he was no longer watching her. She could remember feeling stupid and childish for being disappointed. Why had she been so ready to give in to the overwhelming urge to think up some excuse to seek him out? It was as if she'd been thrown into a time warp. Suddenly she was young and foolish and impetuous again. Asking him if he wanted his tank filled with gas was the only thing she'd come up with. She was glad now that she hadn't had the chance to ask him, she thought venomously. It would serve him right if he ran out of gas on his way home. More important, she hoped she'd learned her lesson once and for all. She knew better than to get carried away with a man's good looks, than to let her emotions take control of her.

Overhearing Jack Reardan's locker-room talk about her didn't upset her nearly as much as the fact that she'd allowed herself to fall into the same old trap. How many times could a heart break before it ceased to function at all? Beth didn't want to find out. It had become quite clear over the years that she and men simply didn't mix well. Like her mother before her, she was destined to spend the rest of her days alone.

Well, not exactly alone. She had Scotty. Beth's heart automatically lightened at the mere thought of her son. Scott was her pride and sole source of joy. His bright, shiny blue eyes and pudgy fingers delighted her as he discovered and learned about the world. His little legs carried him to the far reaches of the backyard, and Beth never felt more needed or necessary than when he turned around to make sure that he could see her and know that he was still safe. His smiles were warmer than sunshine—but they didn't completely fill the emptiness inside her.

It was this hollow, lonely feeling that kept getting her into trouble, she decided, pulling off the main highway onto a tree-lined dirt road that led to her house. Jack Reardan may have been thrilling to look at, with his sandy brown hair and his clear green eyes that twinkled and danced and wrinkled at the corners with good humor, but he wasn't worth risking the pain of rejection. She was sure that his smile could stop a clock, and she wouldn't deny that she liked the way he walked and the way his body seemed so confidently male, but she wasn't a fool anymore. She wasn't about to let her secret needs get the better of her again. And certainly not with Jack Reardan.

Beth drove past her own driveway and continued up the road. The house she had recently bought had been the original McKenzie homestead. Some time ago the McKenzies had outgrown it and had built a larger home farther back in the woods.

Boodle was their oldest child. The youngest wasn't much older than Scott. Jim and Carol McKenzie were devoted parents and very kind people. When Beth had moved in and inquired about day care for Scott, they had insisted she think about leaving him with Carol during the day. "After all," Carol had said with a laugh, "what's one more baby at our house? A little more noise and a lot more happiness." In the end Beth had found the McKenzies and their attitude hard to resist.

The yard, cut out from the dark, dense forest that surrounded it, was lit brightly with floodlights. Douglas firs, ponderosa pines, aspens, junipers, and cottonwood trees had been removed to make way for the cozy log cabin structure that, to Beth, always seemed to be bulging with life and laughter.

She saw Jim stacking wood at the side of the house when she drove up. They exchanged waves, but her eyes were eagerly seeking out her son as three children came running around the opposite end of the house. Eventually, Scott rounded the corner. He propelled himself forward, not really caring where he went as long as the other children were in sight. When he recognized Beth's car, he immediately deviated off course, heading straight for her. They played peek-a-boo through the window for a few minutes before Beth got out and hugged him hello.

"Ms. Simms. Ms. Simms," the other children were all speaking at once.

"Guess what Scotty did today."

"You want to hear somethin' real funny that Scotty did?"

"Watch this, Ms. Simms."

"Who's that? Who's that?" they asked Scott in unison, pointing at their father.

Scotty looked at Jim McKenzie thoughtfully, then he, too, pointed and said very clearly, "Daddy."

"Oh, no, Scott. That's not Daddy. That's Mr. McKenzie," Beth said, trying to hide her embarrassment and correct her son at the same time. "Can you say Mr. McKenzie?"

"It'd probably be easier for him to say Massachusetts," Jim said good-naturedly as he walked over and ruffled Scotty's soft blond hair. He laid his big hand on his three-year-old's head and said, "This one still says he's Todd A-Kenny. And you don't need to feel bad about him calling me Daddy. Everybody does around here. Later on, when he's talking better, we'll start out with Jim, and he can work his way up to Mr. McKenzie."

Beth tried to smile and take the natural misunderstanding in stride, but she couldn't help feeling uncomfortable with it. "I'm sorry."

"Well, don't be. If that's the worst word he picks up around here, we can count ourselves lucky."

Carol came out then with Scott's bag of extras, and after passing a few more minutes of far less awkward conversation with her, Beth took Scotty home.

"McKenzie, Scott. Can you say that?" she coached

him as they drove back down the road toward their house. Night had settled in completely, and total blackness enveloped everything except the road directly in front of them. Her eyes automatically scanned the perimeters for deer, alert to sudden movements of any kind. To hit a deer was one of Beth's greatest fears of night driving.

She had several other fears of doing things at night, but to admit that she was afraid of the dark was ludicrous. Mothers weren't afraid of the dark. "Let's say it together, okay?" she said to her son, using her own voice to distract her thoughts. "Mc-Ken-zie. McKenzie. Now you try it. Okay?"

Scott babbled at her from the backseat as she pulled up in front of her house. Straining her eyes, she scouted the darkness, giving special attention to the area where she knew her trash can stood as an open invitation to hungry bears. Seeing none and praying there was nothing else hidden in the darkness waiting for her, she gathered her courage.

The front porch light glowed like the beacon from a lighthouse that would lead her to safety, but it didn't make the distance she had to travel any shorter. "That was very good, sweetheart. Let's try it again," she said, releasing the latch on Scott's car seat.

"Mc-Ken-zie," she repeated while she waited for the little boy to climb through the bucket seats and join her in front.

"Yite." Scotty pointed to the front porch light.

"Yes. Light. That's good. Let's go turn it off." She gathered her purse, books, and fortitude, and took her son by the hand. With slow, easy steps she walked up the path to the porch.

Once inside, she let Scotty flick the switch to turn

off the light, removed his jacket, and set him free to run wild through the house. Then she leaned back against the locked door and breathed a sigh of relief. It was the little things that reinforced her determination. She was afraid of a lot of things—of raising Scott alone, of not being a good teacher, of not being able to cope with all her responsibilities, of being hurt again and, yes, of the dark. But every time she conquered one fear, she knew she could conquer another. And even as Jack Reardan's face rose defiantly before her, she knew she could overcome the feelings he'd stirred within her. She'd live with the loneliness, and she would tolerate his presence when she had to. She would learn to be impervious to Jack Reardan along with her other fears.

Two

> Amazing grace. How sweet the sound,
> that saved a wretch like me.
> I once was lost but now I'm found.
> Was blind but now I see.

Beth sang along with the congregation, trying to remember how many times she'd stood beside her mother and lifted her voice to the same words. How many times had she looked up at her mother, seeing her as the only constant thing in her life, wishing there were something she could do to make her smile? And later, how many times had she looked over at the woman beside her and understood the misery and bitterness that festered inside her, knowing there was nothing she could do to alleviate it?

Beth couldn't remember a time when her mother laughed for the pure enjoyment of it. She might have been happy as a young bride, in the early years of her marriage, but Beth couldn't remember those years. What she could recall all too vividly were the first few weeks after her father had left them. Beth had waited and waited for him to return. Her mother had given up almost immediately. Beth had hoped and prayed. Her mother had grown cynical and hard-hearted.

Every time she thought of her childhood, it only strengthened her resolve to make sure that Scotty's life would be different. She glanced down at him where he sat in the pew beside her and watched while he made an in-depth study of Big Bird's friend Snuffy. Scotty's life would be filled with joy and laughter. He would know optimism and encouragement. He would remember his mother as being a happy, contented person. This was the vow she'd made to him the day he was born. It was the promise she'd made to herself as a little girl.

Latecomers caught Scott's attention as they quietly took the seats directly behind Beth. He craned his short neck and watched them avidly until they were settled, and then he welcomed them with a friendly "Hi" that echoed through the church as clear as a bell. They must have smiled at him, because he smiled back and raised his hand in greeting. Thankfully, he didn't appear inclined to pursue the relationship at that moment as he amicably complied with Beth's soft "Shh."

Unfortunately, the two-year-old's temperament changed faster than most streetlights. Halfway through the service, the boy came to the conclusion that godliness shouldn't take so long. He began to squirm in his seat and quickly progressed to climbing all over Beth. No sooner had she picked him up, than he wanted to go down again. The pencil and paper she gave him didn't last long, and soon he was hanging over the back of the pew playing pick-up-my-pencil with the people behind them.

Beth made several attempts to distract Scott and keep him seated quietly beside her, but it didn't work. When the congregation stood to sing again, she tried to include him. She lifted him into her arms and made every attempt to draw his attention to the minister at the front of the church, but the people behind them had once again captivated him.

"Daddy." Scotty's voice seemed louder, his words more pronounced as the fading final bars of organ music died. "Daddy."

Beth's eyes rolled heavenward before they closed wearily. Why did three hundred and sixty-five days seem so long sometimes when one was the mother of a two-year-old, Beth wondered, refusing to reflect on the horrors the third year had in store for her. Well, things weren't all that bad, she reconsidered. At least it was Jim McKenzie and his family behind her. They all understood two-year-olds.

There was a gentle clinking of metal before Scott triumphantly dangled a set of keys on a chain in front of Beth's face. "Daddy," he said again, smiling over her shoulder. Beth, grateful for the assistance in keeping the little boy occupied, turned to smile her gratitude at Jim. The smile drooped and froze in a grimace of dismay when her gaze met and locked with Jack Reardan's.

Jack's grin widened, and his pleasure over her *dis*pleasure shone in his eyes. Beth's heart pounded and sank at the same time. There was something exciting about seeing him again, but she had been hoping to avoid him. Her lips wanted to smile warmly at him and whisper a soft greeting, but her mind replayed the incident at the car wash two days earlier. Her heart wanted to forgive him and start all over again, but her defense shields stayed in place when she saw that he was still having a lot of fun at her expense.

"Daddy," Scotty said. Jack chuckled while Beth fought to hide the burning heat in her cheeks. She glanced away only to find Jack's daughter, Chelsea, and an older woman looking on, equally amused.

With great difficulty Beth tried to make the best of the situation. She refused to pass a second glance at Jack, but she did smile stiffly at the girl and the woman. Then she sat Scotty down on the pew beside her and tried to pretend she didn't know to whom he belonged. Staring straight ahead, only vaguely aware of the rest of the service, she reviewed possible scenarios of how she would get out of the church without having to look at or speak to Jack Reardan again. They ranged anywhere from grabbing her baby and running out like a madwoman to evaporating.

While Scotty blissfully kept himself busy trying to unlock her purse with Jack's keys, Beth did her best to keep from fidgeting as she felt Jack's gaze roaming freely over her. It was all she could do to keep from swinging around and slapping him.

As if he sensed that the service was coming to an end and he would soon be free again to do as he pleased, Scotty made an attempt to escape into the pew behind them. Beth thwarted him, dislodging him from the back of the bench. She tried to hold him in her arms until the minister could make his way to the back of the church, where he would greet his flock on their way out.

Scotty apparently had his own social priorities set firmly in his mind. He wanted to get better acquainted with the Reardans, and he didn't want to wait until after the service to do it. He squirmed and flailed until, in frustration, he let out a blood-curdling scream. He held his arms out to Jack saying, "Daddy." Then he turned and bonked his captor on the back of the head with his fist.

Jack couldn't help interfering in the situation. He bent over the back of the pew and took Scott out of his mother's arms.

Beth was more startled and shocked by the feel of his hand wedged between her breast and Scotty's body than she was by Jack's actions. She was speechless as a warm, tingling sensation passed through her when Jack dragged the back of his hand slowly across her breast, taking her son away at the same time.

"Don't you know it isn't nice to hit ladies?" Jack asked Scotty in a firm but not unfriendly voice. "Especially when the lady isn't much bigger than you are. You want to grow up to be a bully?"

The reference to her height was the slap in the face Beth needed to regain her control. In her next life she planned to be tall enough to tell people like Jack Reardan that the part in their hair was crooked.

"He's only two, Mr. Reardan," she said, trying to dismiss the change in the man's appearance. She took in the lack of dirt on his clothes and the absence of fatigue in his face. He'd been transformed from ruggedly handsome into the clean-cut, knock-'em-dead category. His Sunday best fit him perfectly. The fine, dark cloth accentuated his broad shoulders and clung to his thickly muscled thighs. Jack Reardan was stunning. "He's . . . he's just learning to control his temper."

When the minister passed by them on his way out, she expected Jack to give Scott back to her.

Jack, however, was proving to be an unpredictable man. He stepped out into the main aisle and made room in the crowd for his daughter and the older woman to pass by. Then he took a step backward and did the same for Beth.

"I don't think you've met my mother, Ms. Simms. Mother, this is Beth Simms, the new teacher up at the high school," he said, making the introduction over her head. Beth felt his fingers curl around her elbow. She was perfectly capable of finding the front door without his guiding hand on her body, she told him silently by shaking off his light touch.

"I'm glad to meet you, Ms. Simms," Mrs. Reardan said, smiling over her shoulder at Beth. "I've been hearing wonderful things about you from Chelsea."

"She didn't ask my opinion," Jack whispered from behind her, his fingers snaking around her elbow again.

Beth wanted to stomp her feet and scream out loud—but not at Mrs. Reardan. The woman looked like every grandmother ought to. Her light hazel eyes were warm and welcoming, as was her smile, which came easily and naturally to her lips. She was taller than Beth, and her slightly overweight body retained a youthfulness and vigor that belied her gray hair.

"It's a pleasure to meet you, Mrs. Reardan," Beth said sincerely. "And I'm glad the reports are favorable. Hi, Chelsea."

"Morning, Ms. Simms," the girl said, shaking Scotty's arm gently to make the keys in his fist tinkle enticingly. "Your baby is so cute. What's his name?"

"Scott. And believe me, he's had cuter days," she said wearily. Chelsea Reardan was a very pretty girl, in an unassuming way, Beth had noted. Her short dark hair was cut simply and seemed to curl at will. Her eyes, like her father's, twinkled with enthusiasm and intelligence.

"Two-year-olds can be a handful," Mrs. Reardan commiserated as they walked out into the late-morning drizzle. The rain had come as predicted, but had gradually let up during the night and changed to occasional showers. "But take heart, dear, they aren't two forever."

"That's right," Jack agreed, beaming. "Eventually they grow up to be charming, handsome men. Isn't that right, Mom?"

"Yes, dear. Some of them do." The teasing smile she flashed at her son had obviously been passed on to the next generation. He chuckled when Beth slipped him an at-least-your-mother's-no-fool type smirk, then squeezed her arm playfully. Beth glared at him.

They stood together, waiting to speak to the preacher. Acutely aware of how they must look—the kids, the folks, and Grandma—Beth was extremely uncomfortable. She desperately wanted to remove her traitorous son from the irksome man's clutches, but Jack Reardan seemed to know it and was very careful not to let go of Scott. Not that Scotty was protesting. He looked as happy nestled in Jack's arms, surveying the world from a whole new altitude, as any clam Beth had ever seen.

Beth was preparing to make her hasty departure when Mrs. Reardan stopped her. "We usually have breakfast out on Sundays. Would you care to join us today?"

"Oh. Well. Thank you, but I really think I should get Scotty home and feed him some lunch," she said, flustered by the unexpected invitation.

"I think the invitation was for both of you," muttered Jack in a low voice meant only for Beth. Then, in his usual tone, he addressed Scotty. "We can have breakfast, or we can have lunch, huh? Would you like to go get something to eat?"

Scotty indicated that he thought it was a favorable proposition and the matter seemed to have been settled and approved by all—except Beth.

The restaurants in the town weren't noted for their ambiance, but the food was hearty and well prepared in a traditional meat-and-potatoes fashion. Beth, however, was in no mood to enjoy the food. Sandwiched between the two males at a table meant for four, she found herself trying to deal with Scotty's not-yet-fit-for-the-general-public eating habits and Jack's long and suddenly cumbersome legs, which were constantly bumping into or rubbing up against hers under the table.

Added to her problems was the fact that Jack's mother was politely asking the usual getting-to-know-you questions, and Beth was reluctant to reveal anything personal about herself in front of Jack. It soon became a scene she would not soon forget or ever want to repeat.

"What's your choice for the play we'll be doing this semester, Chelsea?" Beth asked during a lull in the conversation, trying to draw the spotlight away from herself for a while.

"*Romeo and Juliet.*" The young girl sighed. Her father's brows lowered into a frown of concern while Beth's rose in interest.

"Have you read it yet? Or are you thinking it's going to be like the movie?"

"Boodle McKenzie and I read it just this summer. We even went into Spokane to see the Interplayers' production of it. It was wonderful."

"Yes, it is a wonderful story. But do you think your classmates are mature enough to pull it off? I mean, sometimes it's hard to get high school students to take drama seriously."

"Last year they did a couple of one act comedies that were pretty good," Jack said, presenting his comment as a suggestion.

"Are there enough students in the drama club this year? There's never been more than a handful that were interested before," Mrs. Reardan asked. She put strawberry jelly on half of a piece of toast and gave it to the baby as if it were second nature to her.

"Well, actually," Beth started, quickly warming to the subject, "since I'm teaching English lit and drama *and* public speaking this year, I thought I could incorporate them. This first semester we'll study Shakespeare in the classroom, and anyone who's interested can join the Drama Club and participate in the production of one of his plays for extra credit. Personally, I think they'll learn a lot more about the history, the play, and Shakespeare if they can really get into it and act it out."

"And they'll also get some exposure to public speaking," Mrs. Reardan added, nodding in approval of the lesson plan. "That's very good thinking, dear."

"Thank you," Beth said.

The older woman looked across the table at her son and frowned. "I don't know what you were so worried about, Jack. I think she's a wonderful teacher. She has a fresh approach and plenty of insight into the age group she's dealing with."

Beth turned in her chair to stare at Jack, who, with his facial expressions, was making a futile attempt to curtail his mother's comments. When he looked down at Beth, he had the decency to appear sheepish. "My mother was the principal at the high school for years. I thought she ought to meet you."

Beth put her tongue in her cheek and considered her next response very carefully. She liked having the upper hand with Jack Reardan. Seeing him embarrassed more than made up for the insult he had just dealt her. She also rather approved of his concern. Not every parent in this day and age thought twice about the kind of teacher his child had, and fewer still would go to the trouble of checking her out.

She relished his discomfort for several more seconds. When she could no longer hide her smile, she turned to Mrs. Reardan. "Well, I hope this doesn't mean I won't be seeing you again. I've very much enjoyed meeting you, Mrs. Reardan."

"Gracious no, dear. We would have met eventually anyway. I'm too old to teach, but they still let me keep my fingers in the pie. And I'll have you know that my minor in college was drama. So if there's anything I can do to help, you can count on me."

"I will. Thank you. And now I think Scotty's played in his food long enough. Thank you for inviting us," she said, and with a direct look at Jack. "We owe you one," she added.

Before making her final exit, Beth took her son into the ladies' room to clean him up. She waved and smiled at the Reardans she liked on her way out the door. The one member of the family she wasn't too thrilled with followed her.

"Beth. Wait up," Jack called from the door. She

turned and watched as he covered the distance of the parking lot in six long, determined strides. He stopped in front of her, looking worried and uncertain. "Look. I'm sorry. I . . . I guess I was out of line, having my mother grill you like that. I apologize."

"Apology accepted." Taking Scott's hand in hers, she turned to leave.

"But . . ."

Facing him once again, she looked askance. "But what?"

"Well . . . is that it? I mean, if you accept my apology, does that mean we're friends? Or at least back to where we started?"

"We started off in the hole, Mr. Reardan. Do you really want to go back to that?" she asked, trying to hold her ground—literally—as Scott tugged on her arm in his efforts to get to Jack.

"No," he said, smiling.

"Let's say we're on equal ground this time and let it go at that."

Oddly enough, the solution didn't seem to please him. "Let it go?"

"Yes. Your mother just told you that I'm not the total incompetent you thought I was. And I don't think you're a complete swine anymore."

"Oh. Well, thank you," he said to Beth's back as she stepped away again to make her exit. This man had such a strange effect on her, she thought. She was being far too easy on him for all his impudence, but she couldn't seem to help herself. In fact, if this were happening to someone else, she might have thought it funny. And there was no denying that he was very appealing when he was contrite. He was appealing physically all the time, she amended to herself, but very appealing emotionally when he wanted to be forgiven.

"But," he said suddenly, "does that mean I'm still too much of a swine for you to consider going out with?"

Sirens and fire alarms went off in Beth's head. She looked back at him in bafflement and with a certain amount of fear. She'd been asked out before since her divorce, but there had always been signals of interest from the man beforehand. It hadn't been difficult to ward off the advances of men who were overly kind and complimentary. Jack's reaction to her could hardly be called kind or complimentary, and his interest in her caught her off guard.

She had been aware of a chemistry between them, and she had never denied that she was attracted to him in a purely physical way. But they'd hardly been affable toward each other. With Jack's sudden about-face, their relationship—past, present, and future—took on a whole new complexion.

To cover her agitation, she struggled to get a still-unhappy Scott into his car seat. "I don't think you're a swine at all anymore, Mr. Reardan. To tell you the truth, I admire the way you acted on your concerns regarding your daughter's welfare. I wish more parents were as diligent."

"Then I'm forgiven for today."

"Of course."

"What about Friday? Are you still mad about that?"

"No. We just got off to a bad start."

"Then you'll go out with me?"

"No."

Jack frowned, confused. Beth finished snapping the straps around Scott, then stood up straight to make her explanation. "I don't think that's such a good idea, Mr. Reardan. This is a small town, and as you said, people talk. I also don't date the parents of my students."

Much relieved, Jack laughed and shrugged off her objections. "That's no big deal. This *is* a small town. If the residents didn't date the teachers, they'd all be spinsters and bachelors. And believe me, people talk a lot more about you if you're not dating than when you are."

"Mr. Reardan—" Beth said, hoping to set him straight before he went any further. But he didn't give her the chance.

"They try to set you up with their second cousin's half sister, and if that doesn't work out, they drag out Aunt Helena's niece by her second marriage. You want that?"

"No." She couldn't stop the soft laugh that escaped her as he shivered at what he obviously considered a plight worse than death.

"You want her nephew?"

"No."

"Well, then you might as well go out with me. We'll protect each other."

"I appreciate the offer, Mr. Reardan, but—"

"And you don't have to worry about Chelsea either. Some of the kids have their own parents as teachers, and they seem to survive." He paused for a brief, thoughtful moment, then added, "Or if you're thinking someone will accuse you of favoritism, well, hell, Chelsea's always been a good student. Let 'em think what they want."

"Mr. Reardan."

"Daddy."

Beth and Jack both turned to look at the single-minded two-year-old who was tired of being overlooked by his newest best friend. "Daddy," he repeated, now that he had their attention.

"Sorry, big guy," Jack said sympathetically. "Mommy

says it's time to go." He stroked Scotty's cheek with his index finger and spoke his thoughts aloud. "It's been a long time since Chelsea called me that. I kind of miss it, you know?"

Beth silently wished he'd kept his thoughts to himself and that her son would soon forget that word. "Mr. Reardan," she said, trying once again to get his attention.

"You know, I think it sounds a little strange for you to be calling me Mr. Reardan all the time while your son calls me Daddy. I'm rather enjoying it, but it's easy to see that you're not. So, maybe if you'd call me Jack, he'd do the same."

"Mr. Reardan," Beth shouted in exasperation. He looked straight at her then with eyes so warm and green, they reminded her of Christmas trees. Beth's breath caught in her throat. Her heart hammered and flopped in her chest like a frightened bird in a wire cage. In that split second she realized that since the moment he'd sat down behind her in church that morning, he had been watching and studying her. There was a gleam of insightfulness in his eyes that told her she hadn't fooled him for an instant, that the information he'd gleaned was considerable and would be put to good use.

He'd known all along she'd refuse to go out with him. He knew the excuses she'd give would be as flimsy as if she'd said she was going to be washing her hair every night for the rest of her life. He wasn't going to make it easy for her to reject him. She grew angry and defensive at his silent intrusion into her character.

"I have to get Scott home. It's past his nap time," she said. There didn't seem to be a need to explain anything, since he already knew most of it. All she could think of was getting away from his knowing eyes. She felt naked and vulnerable and hated him for making her feel that way.

"It's time to let go of the past, Beth. Divorces are always painful, but you have to start living again." His voice was low, full of understanding and compassion. Beth wanted to kick him. She didn't want him to understand her, and she didn't want him to feel anything for her.

"You don't know what you're talking about, Mr. Reardan." She slammed the rear door and got into the front seat.

"Sure I do," he said through the car window, bending at the waist to see her face. "That's why you're running away now. You're afraid to get too close to another man, so you've decided to pretend we don't really exist. And that's okay for now. I'm a patient man. We can have our night out when you're feeling better."

His confidence was irritating. The short fuse on Beth's temper began to sizzle. Her lips curled into a sly smile as she said, "Hold your breath, Mr. Reardan."

Three

> Come, bitter conduct, come, unsavory guide!
> Thou desperate pilot, now at once run on
> The dashing rocks thy sea-sick weary bark!
> Here's to my love!—O true apothecary!
> Thy drugs are quick.—Thus with a kiss I die.

Romeo slumped heavily to the floor beside the lifeless Juliet, and then there was silence.

"Okay, people. I think that's enough for this afternoon. We'll pick it up there tomorrow," Beth called out to her students from her second-row seat in the audience. "And I'd like to see the stage and costume crews for a brief meeting tomorrow at three-fifteen."

The silence was filled by a din of voices and footsteps as thirty-five senior drama students made their way out of the auditorium. Beth said good-bye to those who passed by her on their way out but made no effort herself to leave. She sighed with great satisfaction.

They had been rehearsing *Romeo and Juliet* for

two weeks, and it was going incredibly well. The students were enthusiastic and earnest, showing a decided maturity she hadn't been expecting. There was none of the snickering or giggling she had been prepared to deal with when the star-crossed lovers kissed. And even though the Old English dialogue was a little hard for them to relate to, they all seemed to be trying.

Beth had a feeling that much of the success had to do with the two young people playing Romeo and Juliet. Boodle McKenzie and Chelsea Reardan were naturals for the parts, and they interacted with the same unaffected ease and intensity that real-life Romeos and Juliets had a tendency to use. In fact, if Beth's guess was correct, that's exactly what they were.

There had been no other readers for the lead roles after the two of them had tried out, even though Beth had encouraged several others to audition. And the other students acted as if it was quite normal to see Boodle kissing Chelsea. The thought made Beth chuckle. The two of them might not be star-crossed, but they certainly were mismatched.

Boodle was a big, friendly boy with a C average and a penchant for fast, shiny red pickup trucks, while Chelsea was a soft, pretty, straight-A student who wanted to be a pediatrician. Beth had very few romantic bones left in her body—and those were coated with kryptonite in case some Superman managed to find a chink in her armor. But she had to admit that seeing Chelsea and Boodle together was . . . sweet.

He was gentle and caring and showed an uncommon amount of respect for her. Chelsea was the same toward Boodle, and he seemed to thrive on her attention and thoughtfulness. He lit up like neon every time she looked at him. Oh, to be young, Beth thought with a deep sigh.

"Oh, great. I suppose you're all wrapped up in this *Romeo and Juliet* stuff too," a deep, intimate male voice said from the row of seats behind Beth. She knew the voice too well and had been waiting to hear it again. But it startled her, and she jerked around in her seat to find Jack Reardan lounging comfortably in his. He was grinning and seemed to be enjoying the fact that her cheeks were blazing, that she'd been caught alone with her worst nightmare, a man she was attracted to. "I heard that sigh," he said, cocking a brow. "Were you thinking about me again?"

"Hardly." Beth turned away to hide her face and began to gather her things together. She hated being so transparent to the man. It wasn't fair. And it was extremely annoying.

He'd been on her mind almost constantly since the day in the parking lot when he had asked her out. For the most part, those thoughts had been negative and contemptuous. But late at night, when Beth had no control over her psyche, it ran amok with the fanciful shadows of a man who stirred her emotions and ignited such a burning passion and hunger in her body that she would awake breathless and trembling—and with the distinct feeling that Jack was somewhere nearby. It was unnerving, the way these same feelings churned so easily within her now.

"I tried to talk to you last week at the parent-teacher open house, but every time I thought it was my turn, you went off to talk to someone else. If I didn't know better, Beth, I'd say you were trying to avoid me." He knew as well as Beth did that that was exactly what she was doing. He didn't, however, appear overly concerned with the matter.

"Chelsea is an excellent student, which you already know, so consider yourself talked to, Mr. Reardan," she said. Then, recalling that he was not only a thorn in her side but the parent of one of her students, she started over. "I'm sorry. Was there something special you wanted to discuss with me about Chelsea?"

The glimmer of merriment in Jack's eyes faded and was replaced with a look of gratification and respect as he grew serious and thoughtful. "Yes, actually there is. I need your help with something."

"My help?"

Jack nodded. "Look, I'll get straight to the point here. I . . . I want you to cut Chelsea out of this play."

"But she's Juliet. I can't cut Juliet out of the play."

"No. I mean get someone else to play Juliet."

"But why? She's perfect as Juliet. She and Boodle are so natural together."

"That's the whole point. They're getting a little too natural together, if you get my drift. They spend nearly every waking minute of the day together as it is. This play just keeps them that way. And it's too damned romantic. I don't want all this stuff going to their heads—or to any other parts of their bodies, for that matter."

"What?" Beth was confused. It threw her off balance to have this man acting like a walking, talking ad for heterosexual encounter therapy one minute and a prudish party pooper the next.

"Don't get me wrong," he said, sitting up and

leaning over the back of her seat. "I like Boodle. He's a good kid. I just don't want him for a son-in-law. Not right now anyway. If they're still in love in six or eight years, after Chelsea's had a chance to finish school, I'll be glad to welcome him into the family. But—"

"What on earth are you talking about?" Beth broke in, frowning.

Jack sighed loudly. There was a long pause as he gathered his thoughts and decided where to start to make Beth understand. "I haven't always been a single parent, you know."

"I hadn't for a moment thought that you'd hatched Chelsea, Mr. Reardan." Beth didn't want to hear this. She didn't want to know about his wife. She didn't even want to be in the same room with him. He made her nervous and jumpy. But there was a look in his eyes, a serious, poignant look that kept her there and forced her to listen.

"I was just Chelsea's age when I married her mother," he said, letting go of another long sigh. "It was an unexpected marriage, the result of an unplanned pregnancy. When Chelsea was six months old her mother left. She's a nurse in Boise, with a husband and two other children now."

"I'm sorry" was the only thing Beth could think of to say. Raising a baby alone wasn't easy, she knew. It couldn't have been any easier for Jack then than it was for her now.

"Don't be. It's water under the bridge. What I'm worried about is Chelsea's relationship with Boodle. I don't want history repeating itself. I don't think Chelsea is as gutsy as her mother was. She'd throw away her future, bury her dreams, and stay with the baby."

"The way you did." Beth was surprised at the lack of bitterness and resentment in his tone. He almost sounded as if he admired his wife. Beth wasn't sure what kind of woman would leave her baby. She hadn't been able to when the choice had been hers to make. But she was sure that if another woman's needs were great enough . . .

Jack laughed softly. "You don't need to make me sound like a martyr, Beth. I'm far from it. I love my daughter, but I've also had my regrets over the years. The point here, however, is that I don't want the same thing to happen to Chelsea. I want her to have the choice to be whatever she wants to be. I've watched her and Boodle growing thicker than peanut butter for almost a year now. Every time they go out together, it's like a bad dream for me. I keep waiting for the day when she'll come home to tell me I'm going to be a grandpa."

"That's understandable, Mr. Reardan, but I don't see how I can be of any help to you."

"I want you to help me keep them apart as much as possible. I want you to cut one or the other of them from the cast. If I come home and find them practicing that death scene on my living room floor one more time, there's no telling what I might do." His words were spoken lightly, but his gaze fell away from Beth's as if he were trying to hide his concern. Beth could see that the idea of Chelsea suffering the same fate as her father was very painful to him. "For my part," he said abruptly, "I plan to have a little talk with her. I'll ask her not to see so much of Boodle from now on."

"No! Don't do that," Beth said, instantly on guard and ready to take a stand on the issue. The emotion in her voice gave Jack a start. He stared with open curiosity, and she was hard put to cover up her reaction. "I mean . . . I . . . well, have you given this enough consideration to be aware of all the possible consequences? Some authorities say that separation isn't always the best answer. Sometimes it can be the worse choice, because it only makes them more determined to be together."

"I've heard that one, too, but I know my daughter. If I ask her to stay away from Boodle, she will. She'll be pretty hard to live with," he said with a shudder, "but then again, she might thank me someday."

"I don't think she will, Mr. Reardan." Beth fought to keep her memories deeply buried in her heart, but it was a useless battle. Years seemed to fade away to make the past, and the pain her memories held, a living, breathing thing inside her. She couldn't help the anger she felt, and Jack couldn't help but notice it.

"Well, what do you suggest?" he asked. "I care too much about her just to stand by and watch her mess up her life."

"Who are you to say she's messing it up? There's nothing wrong with being in love, for crying out loud."

"There is if you're too young to know what you've gotten yourself into."

"Chelsea isn't stupid. Why don't you talk to her. Educate her. Let her know how concerned you are. But for heaven's sake, don't forbid her to care about Boodle. You have to be patient enough and trusting enough to let it run its course."

Jack gave her a long, considering stare, during which Beth had time to realize that one of her walls had crumbled, leaving her exposed and vulnerable to him.

"You feel pretty strongly about this, don't you?" he asked, sounding unsure of his previous decision. When Beth nodded emphatically, she watched as his shoulders drooped and he lowered his head dejectedly. He sighed heavily. "Okay. Maybe I should do some rethinking."

Against her better judgment, she felt sorry for him. It was hard to tell how she would feel sixteen years down the road, when she'd be in the same position. Would she be able to stand by and watch Scott heading for one of life's little pitfalls and not make some sort of effort to stop him? She didn't think so.

"I would like to help, though, if I can." Her offer was purely for Chelsea's sake, she told herself. Without her help, Chelsea could wind up like Beth. Alone and lonely. Needy but distrustful. "Do you think it would help if I had a talk with her? I was an eighteen-year-old girl myself once."

"Yeah, right. Yesterday." Jack didn't seem to think Beth could tell Chelsea any more than he already had, and it irritated her. This wasn't the first time he'd inferred that she was as young as she looked. Nor was it the first time she'd wished for crow's feet around her eyes or maybe a tiny little wrinkle someplace to make her look older and wiser. Lord knew, she'd certainly been through enough to earn her fair share of wrinkles.

"I'll admit it hasn't been as long since I was eighteen as it has been for you, Mr. Reardan," she said in a lofty tone, "but there is one other factor here that might make it easier for me to talk to her." Jack's brows rose as he waited for her revelation. "I am a woman."

Jack's slowly changing expression caused Beth

instantly to regret her words. Her heart beat wildly as his eyes greedily took in the evidence that what she said was true. She was a woman. And every feminine instinct she had was telling her to run screaming into the night. Because Jack Reardan was all male, and his instincts were obviously telling him to do something quite different.

"I've noticed that," he said blandly while his eyes twinkled lasciviously. Then he frowned. "Is that why you're avoiding me? Does it bother you that I'm nine years older than you?"

"No." Too late she realized it would have been a wonderful excuse to use. Then again, she thought, he might take to doing jumping jacks in her front yard to prove his virility. No, she decided, the truth was a much better weapon against Jack Reardan. "I'm avoiding you because I don't like you."

"Ah-ha. I have noticed you trying to give me that impression." Jack didn't appear to be particularly upset by this small problem, nor did it keep him from grinning as he got to his feet. The skin along the back of her neck tingled. Beth could feel him watching her as she bent to pick up her things again. She was shaky from the inside out. When she was ready, she turned to him, frowning.

"Do you want me to talk to Chelsea about this or not?"

"I'd appreciate any help you can give me, Beth," he said, smiling, even though his tone was most sincere. "You'll need to spend some time with her, get to know her better, I think, before she'll take you into her confidence. But if it isn't too much trouble for you, I'd be forever in your debt."

"Listen, I'll do it for Chelsea and for no other reason. You don't owe me anything. Okay?"

"Okay," he said with a shrug, following her out of the auditorium. "But I thought I'd be able to return the favor with Scott. Boys his age need a male influence in their life."

"Scotty's doing just fine without a male influence," she said tightly.

"Obviously. That's why he's calling perfect strangers Daddy."

Beth slammed her hand against the bar that released the lock on the door and walked out into the cold October evening. "He's just trying out new words, Mr. Reardan. And words don't always mean much."

"That's true. For example, you tell me you don't like me, and I can see by the way you act that that isn't exactly the case."

She spun around so quickly, she was dizzy for a second. She gasped for air and searched frantically for the words she needed to put the man in his place. "You are the most arrogant, conceited, presumptuous—"

Without giving her the time she needed to gain full control of her senses, Jack literally swept her off her feet and kissed her soundly on the mouth. It wasn't a soft, romantic first kiss either. He kissed like a man who knew what he wanted and what he had to do to get it.

Beth was stunned at first, but it wore off rapidly, and she began to struggle and strike out at him with her fists. He seemed impervious to her blows, except for the tightening of his grip and the increased pressure of his lips. He pulled away briefly, but when she opened her mouth to scream out, he moved in again. His tongue passed by her lips and teeth and went straight for the heart of her.

She grew weak as he sapped her of her life's breath.

He was careful to replace it, however, with a fiery need that started deep in her abdomen and spread throughout her body. He erased all thoughts and memories from her consciousness and then drew pictures of passion and fulfillment on the blank wall in her mind.

Her body refused to defend her any longer. She melted against him, and his grasp became an embrace. She didn't resist when he pressed her pelvis against him, lowered her, and held her close to his desire. Her hands reached out to feel the hard, work-strong muscles of his chest and shoulders. Her lips grew bold, and her fingers felt free to run through his thick sand-colored hair.

It wasn't until she had surrendered completely, revealing her own wants and needs and desires, that he finally ended the kiss and let her slide slowly down his body to the ground. Her toes had barely touched tarmac before she realized what had happened—what she had allowed to happen.

There was no humor in his eyes. Instead, they were gravely serious and reflective, as if more had just transpired than he had planned on. He was looking down at Beth, who still stood motionless in his arms. There was awe in his expression.

"Don't ever do that again," she said breathlessly, her pulse throbbing in her ears.

She could tell by Jack's smug expression that he thought she was a phony. Their kiss made her words a lie. Her chest grew heavy with her guilt. "Okay. I admit it. I'm a little attracted to you," she confessed grudgingly.

"And you're sorry you said you didn't like me," he tacked on to her sentence with a forgiving smile.

"No. I meant that. So this is as far as it's going."

"Ah. More of those words that don't mean much," he said, reaching down to catch a lock of hair that the wind kept blowing across her face, and anchoring it gently behind her ear. "And you're old enough to know better than to use them."

Her emotions were in a state of turmoil. It would be so easy for her to let him kiss her again. He was a wonderful kisser, she thought as she felt her heart race. But he was a man, her mind prompted her, clearing the issue in a hurry. She'd put her faith in men before, and they'd proven to be unworthy. Then again, this was the first time in a long while that she was tempted with the idea of having a man's body close to hers, of being held and whispered to, of kissing. . . . But would it be worth the pain?

She stepped out of his loose embrace and reached for the handle of her car door. "There are a lot of things I'm old enough and wise enough not to do, Mr. Reardan. Letting this go any further is one of them."

With great deliberation and without a second glance at Jack, she secured her seat belt, locked her car door against any and all intruders, and drove away. And even though she knew she'd had the last word with Jack Reardan this time, she was also aware that their encounter was far from over.

Throughout the night thoughts of him plagued her. No matter how she tried, she couldn't block out the memories of his strong arms, the buzzing sensation she'd felt when he'd kissed her, or the way he'd looked at her, as if he knew her so well.

It hadn't occurred to her until he'd told her about his wife that he was her male counterpart—married young, deserted by his spouse, and left to raise a child alone. Only his situation seemed odd to Beth. What kind of man would give up his life to raise his child? What qualities in Jack had possessed him to do it? Obnoxious as he was, she admired whatever it was that had compelled him to keep Chelsea. He had mentioned regrets though. Perhaps his parents had pressured him into keeping her. Beth knew the influence a parent could have in the life of a young adult. Maybe Jack wasn't the saint she was painting him to be. Maybe he hadn't had a choice at the time. Maybe, maybe, maybe. Beth's head was full of questions about Jack. Questions she had no business asking. Questions she wasn't sure she wanted answered.

In Beth's opinion, Chelsea Reardan was one of the most well-adjusted and level-headed teenagers she'd ever met. But she was all too aware that seventeen was a very confusing and trying time of life for even the most clear-thinking of youths. Recurring memories of her own senior year in high school, dredged up by the turmoil Jack Reardan stirred in her heart, compelled Beth to make good on her word to help Chelsea. There was too much potential in the girl to let her make the mistakes her father and Beth had made. If friendship and guidance could keep Chelsea from destroying her future, Beth was more than willing to give both.

The next day at school, despite the reservations she felt about Jack, she made her first attempt to form a bond with Chelsea.

"Sure. I'd love to sit with Scotty. I'll have to ask my dad though," said Chelsea, giving no indication that getting permission would be a problem.

"I'll still be there, of course, but I'd really like to clean out those rain gutters and get some painting done. If I have to stop and climb up and down the ladder every two or three minutes to check on Scott, I'd be at it all day. And this way, the two of you can get to know each other better, and he won't feel strange being left with you later." The plan had come easily. Beth had been thinking for a while that it would be worth a baby-sitter's fee to have uninterrupted time to do some of the work that needed to be done on the house. It would turn out perfectly, she decided.

Four

I have not yet begun to fight!

"Good," Beth said encouragingly to Boodle, who was preparing for a history exam on Monday. She had agreed to quiz him on the material while they worked on her house together. "Just as a point of interest, did you know that John Paul Jones's remains are kept in a crypt in Annapolis? I did a report on him when I was in high school, and that's one of the few things about him that's stuck with me all these years. Isn't it dumb, the things you remember sometimes?"

"I'd be happy just to remember all this stuff until Monday," Boodle said disparagingly.

Beth laughed softly. Cramming for tests was another dumb thing she could easily recall from years gone by. She'd been doing a lot of reminiscing lately. But not today, she told herself determinedly. Not today. "You will. Don't worry. Now"—she paused to look down at the questions in the book beside her—"how long did the American Revolution last?"

She listened to his correct answer and asked the next question, but her mind wasn't on history. She was very much focused on the present and couldn't believe how happy she was to be there.

While Boodle labored on the ground below her, she stood high atop the house with a broom in her hands. She had every intention of sweeping several years of debris out of the gutters that ran the length of the house on both sides. But the dirt wasn't going anywhere. Impulsively, she took her time and allowed her senses to soak in the splendor of what she saw around her.

The woods that surrounded her home were dense with nearly every kind of vegetation imaginable—spruce, larch, and cottonwoods, not to mention the Douglas fir and tall pines part of the state was noted for. Huckleberry bushes were profuse in a couple of secret places she and Scotty had discovered the past summer. They'd even found wild rose and columbine. But with fall, the berries and the buds disappeared, and the color changed as the aspen began dropping its leaves. Beth was sure there was no place as beautiful, whatever the season. And aside from the occasional run-in with Jack Reardan, she couldn't remember ever being so happy or content with what she had.

This is what she had dreamed about. This is what she'd worked so hard for. A home of her own. A safe place where she could raise Scotty without constant reminders of the past. There was no mother to foresee doom and unhappiness in the future. No ex-husband to trip over in the grocery store. There was no one to please but herself, and no one to answer to except Scotty. She was free to be Beth there. Her life was as clean and fresh as the cool autumn air.

Perched on the awning over the far end of the house, removing a hairy bird's nest from the gutter, Beth automatically looked up when she heard the sounds of a vehicle on her isolated road. Her breath caught in her throat when she saw the now-familiar Reardan Logging & Lumber Company pickup pull into her gravel driveway. Her first thought was of her clothes, her old, worn jeans with the hole in one knee and the bulky sweater she'd swiped from her mother's charity box. She barely had time for her second notion—a silent plea heavenward that Chelsea had borrowed her father's truck—when Jack got out on the driver's side.

He shoved his hands deep into his pants pockets and took his time surveying the premises. It was hard to tell what he was thinking from his expression, but there was a definite sense of anticipation about his stance and the way his fingers played with the change in his pocket. Beth could actually feel her temper begin to bubble as she huddled down behind the branches of an evergreen that grew beside the house. She didn't want Jack Reardan hanging around her house. It wasn't part of their deal, and she resented his showing up uninvited.

"Hi, Mr. Reardan," Boodle said as he rounded the corner of the house and spotted the truck. He came into Beth's view momentarily as he walked up to the girl climbing out of the truck. In a completely different tone of voice he said, "Hi, Chels."

"Hi," she said softly, her smile conveying her gladness at seeing him.

Beth watched a frown of confusion and disapproval come and go across Jack's face before he spoke. "How's it going, Boodle? Ms. Simms isn't working you too hard, is she?"

The youth grinned broadly. "No way. I do this kind of stuff at home for free. Getting paid for it makes it a whole lot easier."

Jack nodded his understanding. "From the look of things, she'll end up having every kid in the high school up here helping her. First you, now Chelsea." Beth could tell by the edge in his voice that he was still unhappy with the situation.

"That'd be nice," Boodle said, misconstruing Jack's barbed comment for humor. "She's got a list of things she wants done that's as long as her arm. I can only come to help on Saturdays and Sundays. And with just her and me working, it could take forever."

"Is the place in such bad shape?" Jack asked, frowning openly now as he took a second, more critical glance at the house.

"No. But there's a lot of little things that need doing."

"Like what?"

"Well, today we're doing outside stuff so we can get it done before winter. I'm hanging storm windows. Ms. Simms is cleaning out the gutters and patching loose shingles."

"You mean, she's . . ." Jack's speech trailed off, and his hands flipped out of his pockets as his gaze turned upward to the top of the house.

Caught, Beth felt she had no alternative but to rise to her feet and try to appear as if she hadn't been eavesdropping on their conversation. With a strained smile on her lips she waved. "Good morning," she called, getting the distinct impression she was talking in the past tense as she watched Jack's hands settle firmly on his hips.

"What the hell are you doing up there?"

She looked from Jack to Boodle and back again

before she answered. "Boodle just told you. I'm cleaning the gutters."

"Are you out of your mind?"

"I don't think so."

"Then why isn't Boodle doing that?"

Beth was already weary of the tone of Jack's questions. None of this was any of his business in the first place, and in the second . . . well, just talking to him brought back that nervous, jumpy feeling she hated. She matched his stance before she finally decided to answer him. "Actually, there are a couple of very good reasons why Boodle isn't doing this, Mr. Reardan. One is that the storm windows are too heavy and too awkward for me to handle. And the second reason is that if there are any weak spots in the roof, I don't want him falling through them. Okay?"

"You mean you'd rather fall through them yourself?"

"Not particularly, but I don't weigh as much as Boodle does, and I know what to look for."

"Is that right? And when did you become such an expert on roofing?"

"Since I bought a manual that tells all about fixing your own roof. Satisfied?"

"Hardly," he said, then, turning to Boodle, he asked, "Where's the damn ladder?"

"Don't tell him, Boodle. I don't want you up here, Mr. Reardan." Her words sounded childish, but they were out before she could stop them. An uncontrollable panic rioted within her. She didn't want that man on the roof with her. She wanted him down on the ground and in front of witnesses so he couldn't touch her again.

Boodle stood silent, plainly torn as to which adult to obey. Chelsea was looking anxiously from father to teacher as if they had both suddenly become strangers to her.

"Great," Jack said, throwing his hands up in anger and stalking off to the rear of the house. "I'll just walk around till I find the damn thing."

In a fit of temper every bit as strong as Jack's, Beth released a deep growl. At the same time she stamped her right foot in frustration. It came down hard and went right through the roof, tearing and cracking the surface below.

"Damn and double damn," she muttered as she tried to pull her foot free. When it refused to come loose, she grew warm and feverish in her efforts to conceal what she'd done. She'd rather die than have to admit to Jack Reardan that he was right about the dangers of her being up on the roof. In fact, she'd rather die than have to admit to Jack Reardan that he was right about anything.

She could hear his footsteps as he came toward her from the other side of the roof. In a last-ditch attempt to save her pride, she sat down very gingerly, hiding her foot and the hole in the shingles between her legs.

"I really hope you're not going to give me a bad time here, Beth. I'm not exactly relishing the idea of dragging you kicking and screaming off this roof. But if that's what it's going to take . . ." He didn't finish his sentence. He didn't have to. Beth knew intuitively how it would end. Instead, he lowered himself down beside her and folded his arms around his knees. Looking very content and in no hurry to drag her anywhere, he glanced at the scene below and said, "You know, we could have a nice, private little conversation up here."

"We haven't had a nice conversation since we met,

Mr. Reardan. I see no reason to have one now. Why don't you go home?"

"I don't want to go home. And you have to admit, we've come close to having a decent conversation a couple of times. Maybe if we had a little more practice—"

"Close doesn't win you any cigars," Beth broke in, drawing her thigh closer to the hole in the roof and placing her arms casually around her bent knee to conceal her foolishness. "And in our case, practice could only make things worse. We simply don't get along, Mr. Reardan."

"One of us isn't trying very hard, Ms. Simms," he said pointedly. "However, be that as it may, we do have things to discuss today."

"Such as?"

"Such as why you have Boodle and Chelsea here at the same time. I thought you understood that they were spending far too much time together already," he said so only Beth could hear.

"I also understand that spending time together is par for the course when young people are in love. But I also thought we were going to educate and observe them, not try to keep them apart," she whispered vehemently, glancing down at said young people below. "I'm not going to trick them or deceive them in any way, Jack. I have them both here because I need them both. If we become friends, and they learn to trust me, so much the better. If not, at least we know where they are and what they're doing."

Jack just sat and looked at her for several long, quiet moments before he said, "Say that again."

"What?"

"My name."

"Mr. Reardan," she said automatically.

"You called me Jack."

Beth mentally backtracked over her words even as her skin grew warm under the victorious gleam in his eye. Realizing she had no defense, she stretched her spine to sit a little straighter and with more dignity. "Let's get back to the point, shall we?"

Jack frowned. "What was it? You had me so flustered there for a minute, it's completely slipped my mind."

Beth glared at him. But before she could lash out, their audience was heard from. "Scotty's standing up in his crib and looking out the front window, Ms. Simms. Want me to go in and get him up?" Chelsea asked.

"Oh. Yes. Please." All three of the kids had slipped completely out of her mind. And he said he was flustered. She couldn't let him keep doing this to her. Whenever he was around, he made her so angry and so nervous and so distracted, she could barely remember her own name.

They both watched as Chelsea and Boodle passed out of sight below them, and listened for the front door to close. Beth decided to seize the moment and put an end to this strange power he held over her. She turned to rage at her companion, but Jack was quicker and spoke first.

"Alone at last, huh, Beth?" His grin was sly and calculating and very appealing. He moved closer as he continued to speak. "Now we can let our hair down and just be ourselves. You can be Beth, not the teacher. And I can be Jack, not the dad. Now we can say and . . . do whatever we want."

"Will you stop that!" She put her hands on his chest and pushed him back. Immediately, she wished she hadn't touched him. Her fingers tingled with the awareness of the strength and hardness that lay beneath his soft flannel shirt. Her muscles bunched up, and she pulled away in a reflex action. Jack, again, was faster. He caught her right wrist and held it securely.

"Why should I stop? I'm not getting to you, am I?" He paused and considered her thoughtfully. "Or am I?"

"Like a toothache," she said. Her voice faltered and took a lot of the punch out of her insult. She wanted to kick herself for answering at all.

He placed a kiss in the palm of her hand and another on her wrist above her wildly beating pulse. "I'm not making your heart race, am I? And I'm not making you breathe a little faster, am I?" His gaze dropped to her heaving chest. She suddenly didn't care how ugly the sweater was, she was glad she was wearing it. For him to see how quickly she was breathing was one thing. For him to know that her breasts were engorged from excitement would never do. He gazed deeply into her eyes. "Give me a good reason to stop, Beth." His voice was low and soft like an intimate caress.

A good reason. Beth's mind was a blank. She knew the sun was shining and that a bird was trilling someplacc nearby. The earth was still round and Wednesday always followed Tuesday, but for the life of her, she couldn't think of a good reason for him to stop making her feel so . . . alive.

There was a rebirth of something that had been long dead deep within her. A sense of hope, excitement, and anticipation she hadn't felt, hadn't allowed herself to feel, for a long, long time broke loose inside her. Her spirit began to rejuvenate itself. A buoyancy replaced the heaviness she had carried for so many years. Every fiber, every proton and neutron in her being seemed animated, danced with joy and a desire to live, to touch and be touched by this man. More than anything, she wanted him to kiss her again, to hold her once more. She swallowed hard around the lump in her throat and opened her mouth to speak, but nothing came out.

"Just as I thought," he murmured before his lips touched hers in a light, gentle kiss. Beth's eyes closed. He sipped and tugged on her bottom lip, and things seemed to explode and melt inside her at the same time. Part of her wanted to flop back on the roof and let him take what he wanted. Another part wanted to attack him and take what she needed.

"Now, that's more like it," Jack uttered between kisses. He cupped her face with his hands and deepened each new kiss.

But the satisfied tone in his voice rang like an alarm in Beth's ears. She lowered her face from his and tried to squelch the confusion and pain that began to play over and over again in her mind. She was, once again, the little girl promising to be very, very good if only her daddy would come back to her. She was the child full of guilt and anguish whose prayer was never answered. She was the young woman defying her mother, risking her future and the only home she'd ever known in the name of love. She was the pregnant woman, alone and frightened and betrayed. . . .

"Beth?" Jack's voice was gentle and concerned. It touched her, and she recoiled defensively like a wounded animal. "Do you want to talk about it?"

She shook her head.

"It might help. I've been through it. You really shouldn't keep it all bottled up."

"It's not bottled up," she said, unable to stop the overflow of emotions that came pouring out of her. "If I could bottle it up, I might be able to ignore it, pretend it never happened. But it's like an open wound. Always there and always painful."

"It'll heal. I promise."

She shook her head again. "I don't think I want it to. I want to remember. I don't want to make the mistake of trusting someone again." With that said, she felt she should look at him, let him see how serious she was. Surely then he would understand and leave her alone.

If he saw her determination, he didn't appear to be put off by it. She watched as the expression in his eyes grew soft and tender and solicitous. He looked sincere, as if he truly cared and wanted to soothe her. But she didn't want him to bother with an attempt at being kind. He'd already gotten closer to her than she had intended to let anyone get again. "I don't want another man in my life. Not now, not ever. I wish you'd just stay away from me."

Her blunt words didn't change his demeanor as much as she had hoped they would. He didn't look insulted or angry or hurt. In fact, he didn't appear the least bit discouraged. She was beginning to wonder what she was going to have to do to get the message across, when he finally spoke.

"Whoever hurt you did a bang-up job of it," he said, more to himself than to Beth. His gaze wandered freely over her face as if it had become something very familiar and special to him. "If you want me to stay away, I will. I can't promise that I'll duck out of sight when I see you coming or that I won't go out of my way to be someplace where I think you might show up though. And I don't know how long

I'll let you keep me at arm's length. But for now I'll do as you ask—on two conditions."

The man had more nerve than poodles had curl, Beth marveled as she sat waiting for him to continue —and she was sure he would go on to deliver his terms as if the situation were negotiable. Under other circumstances she might have laughed at his audacity, but these were not other circumstances. She was perfectly serious, even if he chose not to believe her.

"First, I want you to think about something," he said slowly, choosing his words carefully. "I'm not the guy who hurt you. I'm not anyone you've ever met before." He paused. "I'm not saying that you and I ought to run off and get married, but I think there's something special between us that we ought to investigate. I think we owe it to ourselves to make sure that we're not throwing away something very vital in our lives."

"We hardly know each other," Beth said, refusing to acknowledge the way her words stuck in her dry throat or the way her heart was hammering painfully in her chest. "And I don't—"

Jack placed his index finger against her lips to silence her. "I don't expect you to admit to feeling it. But I know you do. That's why I scare you. You want to know me better, but you're afraid I'll hurt you. I understand that. So, I'll give you some time to realize that it isn't fair to use some other guy as a ruler to measure me. But it's not always going to be like this, Beth. I think we're going to find that this thing is bigger than both of us."

The tone of his voice wasn't threatening. He was simply stating the facts as he saw them. Beth heard some truth in his words and cringed inwardly at the implications.

"And what exactly is it that makes you so different from other men, Jack?" she asked tauntingly, even though she felt his answer would have the power to seal her into a tomb of bitterness and despair forever. "I didn't just wake up one morning and decide to live the rest of my life alone, you know. It wasn't something I decided to do yesterday. I've had almost three years to make up my mind. Almost three years to rebuild and start a new life for Scott and me. Why should I believe anything you say?"

There was a flash of something—interest or maybe realization—in Jack's eyes before he glanced away briefly, as if searching for the right words to explain himself. Beth remained silent, conscious of the fact that she was watching him intently for the slightest hint of falsehood in what he was about to say.

But when Jack spoke again, his words were strong and heartfelt. "I believe in things, Beth. Marriage, parenthood, commitments, responsibility. These are important things to me. They've always been a part of my life, given it direction and made it worth something." He took a deep breath and shifted his weight, showing his discomfort at speaking so openly about the essence of who he was. Still, he went on. "After my wife left, I could have left Chelsea with my parents and let them raise her. At eighteen I was tempted by the idea. And I hate to say it, but I even thought about putting her up for adoption. But I didn't. And it wasn't just because I loved her. It was because she *was* everything I believe in. The minute I saw her, I knew I'd never be able to forgive myself if I turned my back on her."

Beth didn't know what to say. She wished it were her father or her ex-husband speaking the words. Her life would have been so different if it were. But it wasn't her father and it wasn't her ex-husband speaking. It was Jack Reardan.

"Come on, let's go," he said, getting to his feet, extending a hand to help her up. He didn't seem to need or want her to comment on what he'd just said. She'd asked, he'd answered. It was that simple to him.

Beth was ready to follow him down off the roof. The magic of the day was gone, and the wind had picked up, blowing cold through her sweater, settling close to her bones. Then she remembered why she'd sat down in the first place. The splintered wood around the hole in the roof scratched at her ankle when she moved it to see if it was still as tightly stuck as before. Her life hadn't exactly been charmed of late, she decided gloomily.

"You go ahead. I still have some things to finish up here," she said with a small, tight smile.

Jack shifted his weight and smiled down at her indulgently. "You haven't asked what my second condition is yet."

"I didn't exactly ask to hear the first one."

"If you want me to leave, you're going to have to agree to both of them, or the deal's off. I'll spend the day."

"Well, I do want you to leave. So spit it out."

"You have to get down off this roof and stay down. I'll finish up here for you."

"You're leaving."

Jack's eyes narrowed slightly, gauging her stubbornness. "Okay. Then you let Boodle do it. At least he knows what he's doing. How-to book or no how-to book, patching a roof isn't a woman's job."

The feminist in her came to the surface. She was about to tell him what he could do with his antiquated ideas about women, when she noticed how grim his expression had become. He looked like a soldier prepared to go to war. And if push came to shove, Beth had the feeling that even if she won the argument, he'd throw her over his shoulder, and she'd lose this battle. Besides, getting him out of her life took priority over saving her pride, she decided. She could back down and agree to this concession. She hadn't been too excited about patching the roof anyway. "That's the dumbest thing I've ever heard," she said, unable to give up gracefully. "But if that's what it's going to take to get you out of my hair, I'll come down."

Jack offered her his hand again. And once again she had to decline it. "That's okay. I can manage. You go ahead and I'll follow you. I have to pick up my broom and Boodle's book and . . ."

He bent over and picked up her things. This time when he extended his hand she had the choice of making a fool of herself by refusing to take it, or making a fool of herself by taking it, getting up, and revealing the hole in the roof. Either way the moment promised to be a difficult one.

Resigned to her fate, she wasn't about to compound the awkwardness by touching him. She'd get up without his assistance, she decided, leaning forward and pushing herself up off the roof with her hands. The ground below rushed up to meet her when she looked down at it. It startled her. She lost her balance and swayed precariously over the edge of the roof. She screamed, but all that came out of her mouth was a tiny, weak cry for help.

Suddenly she was upright and safe—relatively safe. She hadn't heard Jack drop the things he'd been holding, but he was holding her now, close and possessively. She pressed the side of her face against his chest. She could hear his heart thumping. It matched the cadence of her own pulse as it shook her body with each enlivening beat.

"You okay?" he asked.

Beth nodded and looked up at him. Above the fearful and deeply intense green eyes; above the sandy brown hair that ruffled gently in the wind, there was nothing but bright blue sky—clear sky, with no beginning and no end, no future and no past. It was like standing on the brink of infinity, and all she could think about was how secure and warm she felt in Jack's arms. Time isolated itself, and nothing was more important than that single second of oneness they shared.

It was only a split second, however, and it might have gone by unnoticed, except that both of them were acutely aware of its passing. Jack looked as if he had been about to step into her soul, to discover the secret of who she was and claim her as his own. But suddenly the moment was gone, the portal closed. Beth felt as if she were beating on a closed door trying to get out—then realized the hopelessness of her efforts. If Jack had managed to get in, or if she had somehow been able to overcome the barriers she'd built to protect herself, the end would be the same as always. Beth would suffer.

There was a look of regret in Jack's eyes as he slowly eased away from her. His hands remained on her shoulders. He seemed reluctant to release her. Beth felt sick and empty. It was a sensation she was all too familiar with, and one she didn't particularly like. She hated it, in fact. She wanted to fill herself with love and happiness and contentment. She could recall these emotions very well and wished she dared to feel them again. But life had proven to her that they didn't last long. They were precursors to pain, disappointment, and despair. Jack wasn't the only one who regretted that things between them couldn't be different.

He smiled at her briefly, trying to lighten the mood. She watched as he distanced himself. It was as if he had physically moved away from her, and yet he hadn't budged an inch. "That was close," he said in a strange voice, obviously ill at ease. "Very close."

His right hand moved down to her elbow as he started to lead her away from the edge of the roof and back toward the rear of the house, where the ladder stood propped against the side. When she didn't follow his lead, he looked back at her. His gaze slowly traveled the length of her body until he discovered the cause of her hesitancy.

Beth glanced down at her foot and vaguely wondered if she looked as stupid as she felt. She speculated on the possibility of pretending she hadn't noticed what she'd done until now. When she couldn't put it off any longer, she glanced up to find Jack with his tongue in his cheek trying very hard not to laugh.

"Don't you dare say it," she said, frustrated beyond belief.

"What? I came all the way up here, saved your life, and now you're going to refuse me this one small reward?"

"Don't say it, Jack." Despite her embarrassment, Beth felt laughter welling up inside her. She tried to scowl and keep her lips from twitching into a smile, but it soon became a futile effort.

"You're a cruel woman, Beth Simms," he said as he bent to help her dislodge her foot. Jack shook his head at his overestimation of her. "Opportunities like this don't come along every day, you know. Come to think of it, if our positions were reversed, how do I know you wouldn't jump at the chance to say it to me?"

With both feet on solid surface, Beth watched Jack's tall, lean body straighten to an upright position, saw the merriment in his eyes, and laughed at his struggle to contain himself. She stretched the cramped muscles in her leg and tried to look innocent. "Me? I'm far too sweet a person."

"I'd be an idiot to pass this up. I gotta do it, Beth," he said, not sounding the least bit sorry. Her innocence and sweetness fazed him not in the slightest.

It occurred to her that it had been a long time since she had enjoyed such silliness with someone. It felt good, and she couldn't see any harm in letting it go on.

"Okay. Do it and get it over with, Jack," she said, making her best attempt to sound annoyed, looking away to hide the smirk on her face.

Jack looked like a kid on his first trip to Disneyland. He spread his arms out wide, tossed back his head, and shouted, "I told you so!"

Beth laughed with him. And she was all too aware of how wonderful it felt.

Five

I can't sleep.

"So?" Beth asked, feeling no guilt at sounding so rude and uncaring. There hadn't been the slightest doubt in her mind as to who would have the nerve to call her so late at night. She wasn't even sure why she'd answered the phone. But she was fairly certain that the rush of excitement she'd felt when the phone rang had been fear rather than any desire to talk to Jack. She hadn't wanted the sound to startle Scotty and wake him up. *That's* why she answered on the first ring. She wasn't in the least bit eager to hear Jack's voice, she told herself.

"So I thought maybe you'd be a little restless tonight too."

"Why would you think that?" she asked, playing with the filmy layer on the top of her third cup of warm milk. "I worked myself ragged today. I'm exhausted."

"Then why are you still up?"

"Who said I was?"

"You answered the phone pretty quick for someone who was fast asleep."

"I'm a light sleeper, and I didn't want you to wake up Scotty," she said. She knew the excuse would come in handy sometime. She hadn't done a very good job of deceiving herself a few seconds earlier, but she might get away with it on Jack.

"Actually," he said in a voice that was suddenly low, lazy, and lascivious. "I was hoping to catch you in bed. We can turn out our lights and talk softly, as if we'd just finished making love. Do you like to whisper in the dark after sex, Beth?"

"You'll never know, Jack," she said, her voice soft and secretive. She knew she ought to hang up on him. This wasn't the sort of conversation one allowed to continue if one had no intention of developing a relationship that involved more than social tolerance. But there she was, Beth Simms, her heart racing, a gentle curve on her lips as she flicked off her bedside lamp.

"I keep thinking of the kiss we shared this morning," he said softly, knowing he had her attention.

"Oh?"

"Mmm. I've been lying here trying to remember the last time a kiss excited me the way that one did."

"And you called to tell me?"

"No. I called because I wanted to hear your voice. I wanted to talk to you."

"But what about the kiss? Have you been kissed like that before?" Beth cringed as she heard her words echo back to her. What a stupid question to ask. She didn't really want to know the answer.

Jack would think she'd enjoyed the kiss and was fishing around for his reaction—which she was, she realized reluctantly. The truth was, she'd been wondering all night. She'd gone to bed three times determined to sleep, only to toss and turn, recalling Jack's kiss and wondering if he'd been half as affected by it as she had been.

There was the briefest of pauses before he said, "Never," in a way that left no doubt about his honesty. Still, Beth had conditioned herself to be wary. "Which is why I'm still awake and thinking of you. I want to know all about you. Who you are. What you like. What you think about. Beth, there's so much we don't know about each other."

"I . . . I thought we had decided to steer clear of each other. I mean, you did promise to go away and leave me alone. I thought you understood that I don't want you in my life."

"Well, I've been thinking about that too," he said in earnest, sounding like a man who had come to some conclusions and felt pretty sure of himself. "First off, I promised to leave. I didn't promise not to call you. And second, I think all that stuff about not wanting me in your life is an emotional reaction against getting hurt again. I don't think you really mean it."

"What!" Beth gasped. She had meant it. She truly didn't want Jack anywhere near her. He scared the livin' bejeepers out of her, because part of her wanted him to be so close to her that they'd look joined at the hip. That part of her wanted to reach out to Jack, wanted to open up to him and show him who she was inside. It wanted Jack to be pleased with what he saw. It wanted him to care about her, love her, take and hold her. It didn't want Jack ever to let go. But what if he wasn't pleased? What if it wasn't enough to make him want to keep her? What if he got tired of her and threw her away? What if . . . "Who do you think you are, talking to me like that? I know what I mean and what I don't mean when I say something. Really. You have a lot of nerve."

"Yeah, I do. And aren't you glad? Otherwise I might have believed you."

"Jack," she said on sigh.

"What?"

"What am I going to do with you?" The question was directed more at herself than at Jack.

"Give me a chance."

"No."

"Talk to me."

"No."

"All right, then, just listen. That won't hurt you. I'll talk, you listen, and before we know it, you'll figure out that I'm not such a bad guy after all and that you can trust me."

"This isn't a good idea, Jack."

"You got a better one?"

"You've heard mine." Beth could feel herself slipping over to his side. Her voice didn't hold the conviction it once had.

"That's not better. That's dumb."

"I still don't want to see you. I don't want you hanging around my house and showing up every time I turn around."

"Well, if you're going to be stubborn, I guess I'll keep my job and carry on some semblance of living my usually very busy life," he said facetiously, making Beth feel small for her rudeness. "But we can at least talk, right?"

"What about?" Beth asked, indulging her weaker side by giving in to Jack. It jumped with joy and warmed her from the inside out. She snuggled down into the blankets and almost giggled like an adolescent. Lord, it was as if she'd never talked to a man on the phone before, she thought, very aware that she was feeling no remorse. It felt good to be young and excited and full of anticipation again, even if it was just for one night.

"Well, since you're still a little touchy, we can talk about me. Anything special you want to know?"

"No," she lied, automatically keeping her front up in case she was making a mistake. What she really wanted to know about Jack was . . . everything.

"Okay," he said in a tone of voice that all but called her a liar. "I'll start at the beginning, and if you have any questions as I go along, feel free to jump right in. Okay?"

"Okay." Beth smiled, glad that sometimes Jack knew she didn't always mean what she said.

"I'm a terrific person. You can ask anyone in town—if you haven't already. They'll tell you I've lived here all my life, that I'm honest, trustworthy, and loyal. They'll also probably tell you that I was born while my dad was snowed in up in a line shack. My mother says it was the worst and the best night of her life. . . ."

Six

I'm innocent.

Jack was speaking aloud as he drove south on the highway Friday morning, heading for his office. "I'm not perfect, but I'm not exactly the scum of the earth either," he said, defending his position in a heated, ongoing discussion he'd been having with himself for the past week. He knew in his heart that he hadn't done anything wrong. He'd made his mistakes, certainly, but he was innocent in this case, and he resented the man whose crimes he was paying for—that invisible, unknown man who had once been married to Beth Simms, that shadow of a being who'd fathered her son. Jack wanted to wring his neck.

What kind of a lowlife would have used her so badly? What had he done to her? How had he inflicted wounds that refused to heal? And how on earth was Jack going to get through to her?

A week had passed since the morning on the roof.

He'd called her late every night, so they could converse without interference from Chelsea or Scotty. He'd talked until he was nearly blue in the face, and Beth had listened, even asked a couple of not too personal questions. But he wasn't any closer to her than he had been a week before.

He'd even kept his end of the deal. He hadn't tried to see her, not up close anyway. Parking across the street from the school and waiting for her to come out didn't count as seeing her, did it? he wondered. In Jack's book, seeing her meant being close enough to touch her, to watch the expression in her eyes change, to smell her sweet, musky perfume. Watching her from afar simply didn't cut it. It was like trying to put out a forest fire with a glass of water. What he needed was a good drenching. What he wanted was to submerge himself in her presence. There was no doubt about it. In Jack's mind, promising to keep his distance was one of the dumber things he'd done as an adult.

Having had six days to reconsider his hasty decision to play things her way—which wasn't getting them anywhere—Jack had decided to test the water, so to speak. After all, how else would he be able to judge whether or not she'd been holding up her end of the deal? How would he know if she'd been thinking about him, about the kind of man *he* was, if he couldn't look into her eyes? He was tired of talking and not being able to see if he was making any difference.

Beth had asked Chelsea to come over on Saturday to help her again, and Jack had jumped at the chance to drive Chelsea there on his way in to the office to do some catch-up work.

They arrived to find the yard empty but soon discovered the place was far from deserted. Jack got out of the truck and was met by a blast of rock 'n' roll music that nearly knocked him over. The little house was practically pulsating as a heavy bass rhythm blared from within, vibrating the windows and scaring every bird within fifty miles.

"Sounds as if Boodle's already here," he muttered absently as he waited for Chelsea to catch up with him. A glance in her direction confirmed that the news wasn't a disappointment to her. Her smile was broad and anticipatory, much like the one Jack wished he could be wearing. The fact of the matter was, Jack was scared spitless. His mouth was dry and his heart was pounding. Lord, you'd think he'd never seen a woman before, he admonished himself.

Their first knock wasn't answered. Jack beat on the door and was surprised when a young girl of eleven or twelve with braids and braces opened it. He recognized her as one of the McKenzies, but he wasn't sure if her name was Allison or Mary.

"Hi, Mr. Reardan. Hi, Chelsea. Come on in," she said, looking very comfortable playing the hostess. "Boodle's in the kitchen," she hollered over the music. "And Ms. Simms is up in Scotty's room. But he's down here with us so he won't be in the way."

The amenities apparently over, the girl turned and went into the living room to join what appeared to be the rest of the McKenzies, save Boodle and his parents. She scooped Scotty up and twirled him around and around until he let loose a screech of glee.

"Thanks for the ride, Dad. I'll see you later." Chelsea's kiss on Jack's cheek was pure reflex, he decided when she left him in search of Boodle. She didn't give him a backward glance or a second thought. He couldn't help missing the old days, when she'd cried every time he left the house.

Jack stood in the small entrance hall for several minutes. He knew he should leave, but he didn't want to. Even the loud music didn't dampen his desire to see Beth. The stairwell was only six feet away, and the temptation was too great. He had to see her. He had to talk to her. He didn't want to live through another week like the past one.

When he reached the top of the stairs, there were only two rooms to choose from. The room on his right looked to be Beth's room. There was a paper-cluttered desk against the far wall, a sewing machine, several unpacked boxes, stacks of books, and a double bed squeezed into the small space. No wonder Jim McKenzie had moved out, Jack thought absently as he turned in the opposite direction, looking for Beth.

Scotty's room was on the left at the top of the stairs, and at the moment it was getting a fresh coat of bright orange paint. Jack stopped dead in his tracks. Under normal circumstances, the color of the paint alone would have been enough to make him stop and catch his breath. But it wasn't the paint so much as the painter that got to him.

Beth, in a white T-shirt and the same tight jeans with the hole in the knee that hadn't gone unnoticed by Jack last weekend, was busy painting. He had expected to find her painting. What he hadn't expected was to see the dreamy, faraway expression on her face or to find her bobbing and swaying to the music in a way that made his eyes bug out and his mouth drop open. He gripped the door jamb for support as her hips undulated, her knees bent, and her torso curved and twisted in the most exotically erotic movement he'd ever seen.

Jack swallowed hard. This was no time to act like an animal. He was positive that Beth wouldn't appreciate being thrown to the floor and ravished. He had a feeling that that was exactly what he ought to do to get her attention but decided to save it as a last resort. Instead, he tried to look relaxed, amused rather than half crazed with desire. He watched her and wondered if she was double jointed when she bent to fill the paint roller without missing a beat.

Beth finished the section of wall she'd been working on and set the paint aside to move the drop cloth over to the next section. With her hands on her hips, she stepped back to survey her efforts. She came within three feet of him before her sixth sense kicked in to tell her she wasn't alone.

Immediately she looked flustered and ill at ease. It wasn't the reaction Jack had been hoping for. "Oh. Hi. I didn't know you were there. How . . . how long have you been standing there?"

Jack knew her mind was reviewing her actions over the past few minutes. He could tell she'd be embarrassed if she thought he'd seen her dancing. And he didn't want to make things worse. "I just got here," he said, his voice loud enough to be heard over the music. "I brought Chelsea and thought I'd stop to say hello."

Beth nodded. It was difficult for him to determine what she was thinking as she stood staring at him with those big gold-green eyes but it wasn't hard to tell that she hadn't had a change of heart about him. She was as wary and defensive as ever.

"Bright color." He tilted his head toward the wall, wishing he had more to talk to her about.

"They say that you can actually raise a child's IQ by surrounding him with bright colors. Not that I'm worried about Scott's, but it can't hurt. And I like bright colors. When I was growing up—" She stopped herself, looking away from Jack. She wouldn't even share her childhood with him, he noted, feeling hurt and disgruntled.

"I see you've accumulated a few more recruits. If the music doesn't shake the house down, you'll have things shipshape in no time."

"I'm baby-sitting," she shouted back at him. "The McKenzies have gone into Spokane for the day. I needed Boodle, so I asked the younger children to come over and play with Scotty. That way Jim and Carol won't have to worry about them."

Jack stepped farther into the room and closed the door, which acted as a partial buffer against the blaring music from below. "I can see why they went. I'm surprised they don't go more often if it's always this noisy at their house."

"I don't think it is," she said, casting a leery eye at the closed door. "The kids were a little surprised when I allowed them to play the music so loud. But it's not hurting anyone, and I like the noise."

"I can't even hear myself think."

"Maybe that's just as well." Her response was impulsive, he could tell by the reluctant smile that crept across her lips. His heart lurched, and a ray of hope shone down on his gloomy prospects for their relationship. Humor was a start, a good start. And she hadn't thrown him out on his ear yet. That was another good sign.

Jack returned her smile with more confidence. "Maybe," he conceded.

The term *lapse in conversation* didn't do justice to the strained atmosphere between them. The only safe topics that remained were politics, the weather, and the attraction they had for each other. Jack didn't think it was the right time to launch into a political discussion. Talking about the weather would seen too obvious a ploy. And their attraction . . . well, they'd been communicating their feelings on the subject from the very start—on a nonverbal level.

Jack walked slowly around the room, pretending interest in the bright orange walls. Beth circled in the opposite direction, keeping the distance between them at a maximum at all times. The music still roared from below. Jack could feel the floor vibrating under his feet. But in Scotty's half-painted bedroom, no words were spoken.

"I guess . . ."

"Why . . ." They began at once, breaking under the tension at the same time. They smiled politely at each other and insisted the other go first simultaneously. Beth gave in.

"I guess you're glad it finally stopped raining," she said, choosing the most detached topic.

"Yeah. It makes getting the logs out a lot easier."

"What happens when it snows?"

"We close down most of the logging operation and run the mill like crazy until spring."

"What happens to the loggers? Are they out of work all winter?"

"No. We take them on at the mill. We plan it that way. Production at the mill is cut back in the spring, and the loggers go back up into the mountains."

Jack's answers were short and recited by rote. He didn't want to talk weather and work. He wanted to talk about Beth.

"This being a logging town and all . . ." Her words trailed off as she realized how inane they sounded. She lowered her gaze uncomfortably and shifted her weight from one foot to the other. "I suppose your house is quiet. I mean, with just you and Chelsea there, there probably isn't much noise."

Jack frowned at her abrupt change in conversation, but it was as close to a personal question as she'd ever gotten, and he was eager to answer. "It's not exactly a tomb, but it's not this noisy, no. Why do you ask?"

"I was just wondering."

"Why?"

She shrugged. "My house was always very quiet when I was growing up. I like the noise."

A revelation. A personal confidence—of sorts. Jack was thrilled. "What color was your room?"

"White with pink accents. And clean. My mother was a very clean person."

"Is she still living?" Jack felt like a salesman with his foot in the door, trying to get all the information he could before it was slammed in his face.

"Oh, yes."

"Do . . . ah . . . the two of you get along?"

"Sure. We're just different, that's all. I like noise and bright colors, and she doesn't."

Jack nodded his understanding. and found himself at a dead end in his line of interrogation. He didn't know where to go from there. But Beth seemed to be in an open, talkative mood, and he sure didn't want to blow his chances.

"How did your husband feel about noise?" Too

late, Jack knew he'd asked the wrong question. Beth's defensive shield shot up, and they regressed back to silence for several minutes. "I'm sorry. I thought you were ready to talk."

"About my ex-husband?" The expression on her face was reproachful.

"Well, I'm tired of paying for his sins and not knowing anything about him or what he did," Jack blurted out in frustration.

"Don't be ridiculous. You're not paying for anything."

"The hell I'm not. You won't have anything to do with me because he hurt you. And it's not fair."

"Fair? What's fair, Jack?"

"Fair is not judging me by his sins. Fair would be to see me for who I am instead of constantly comparing me to him." He took a deep breath and continued. "Has anything I've said all week gotten through to you? Made any difference at all?"

"Not really." She was a picture of defiance, standing there with her jaw set and her body rigid. Jack wanted to shake her. How could anyone so adorable be so stubborn, he wondered. Well, she'd have to give in eventually. He was beginning to think that the rest of his life depended on it.

Wordlessly, he watched as she silently dismissed him and returned to her painting. She had the practice of ignoring him down to an art form—and nobody ignored Jack Reardan.

"Okay, Beth," he said, walking up behind her, his voice reasonable and calm despite the chaos his emotions were in. "Don't listen to me, don't believe anything I say. Keep yourself wrapped up in your protective cocoon. I know what you're feeling, and if you want to do this the hard way, we'll do it the hard way. If you want to play the martyr, fine. Play the martyr." Jack took Beth by the arms and turned her around to face him. He wanted to make sure she heard the rest of what he had to say. "But I'm not going away. You can pretend I don't exist. You can go on taking your anger out on me if that's what you need to do. But I'm not going to just lie down and die because of something someone else did to you. I feel things for you that I've never felt for another woman, and I'm not about to give up on them. Do you hear me? I'm not going to give up on you, Beth. You can't hold out on me forever. And believe me, I'm not above going through all this with you if that's what I have to do. Because when it's over, I have a feeling I'll be glad I did."

Beth was frowning when he left her. He wasn't sure if she was angry or confused, but he was sure that she'd heard him. The question now was, did she believe him? He hadn't meant to be so blunt or sound so uncaring about her feelings. But he'd felt so ineffective and so insignificant to her, the words had just spilled out of his mouth.

There was something about that pigheaded, feisty little woman that brought excitement and awareness back into his days and nights. She was so full of zeal and energy. It was tearing him apart to watch her strangling the life out of her own existence, denying herself the happiness and contentment she could find if she weren't so afraid of dealing with the past and letting herself be herself.

And it was becoming clearer to Jack that she hated the prison she'd locked herself into. It seemed as though every time Jack talked to her, she managed to let something slip by her defenses, almost like a cry for help. She refused to openly expose herself to him, but in a fit of anger she had revealed that she'd been divorced for almost three years. Jack wasn't stupid. If Scotty was two, that meant her husband had left her alone and pregnant. She'd mentioned her mother, but she hadn't mentioned a word about her father. So what about her father? Had he walked out on her too? Repeatedly she'd told him that she didn't want or need a man in her life. But she did. Every time he kissed her, every time he touched her, every time he got within ten feet of her, she conveyed a need to be held and cherished.

"Damn and double damn," Beth swore angrily, watching through the upstairs window as Jack left. He looked upset as he got into his truck, slammed the door, and drove off in a rush. The truck disappeared among the trees within seconds, leaving Beth with a flat, deflated feeling in her chest.

Why had she treated him like that? Why hadn't she talked to him, told him how she was feeling? Why had she been so afraid of him that simple speech had been impossible? She hadn't meant to ignore him. She just didn't know what to say, where to start to tell him that if he was still willing to try a relationship with her, she was willing too. Now it was too late. He was furious with her, tired of putting up with her insecurities and her defensiveness. Now he was gone, and for all his impassioned words, he would probably think long and hard before he returned. After all, how much could one man take?

She knew the answer to that question. She'd already had two men walk out of her life with far less cause than Jack had. She turned back to the room and listened as Jack's words echoed through the emptiness.

The room was gloomy. No longer could she see the bright, cheerful orange paint on the walls. Instead, she saw a dingy, colorless white, devoid of any life or vibrancy. They were very much like the walls she'd grown up with in her mother's house. Beth was suddenly aware of an ominous feeling that permeated the house like the stench of something dead or dying. Her chest grew tight, and she couldn't breathe. She was overcome by a terrorizing fear that she was back in her mother's drab, empty house. In a conscious nightmare she became her mother, full of bitterness and suspicion.

"Oh, Lord," she whispered as the dream passed slowly away and realization set in. It was true. It was all true. She was turning herself into an exact replica of her mother. A lonely, empty shell of a woman who had buried her love so deep that she couldn't feel anything anymore.

Her mother never laughed, never cried. She didn't cuddle with Scotty or encourage him in his silliness. She had no friends, no life outside her job. Her mother didn't live, she wasn't really alive. She simply existed, waiting to die. She was everything Beth had always vowed never to be.

Her body shook convulsively at the picture she had of her life, of the life Scotty would have to live if she didn't break the pattern. And she wanted to break the pattern. More than anything else in the world, she wanted to be alive. Even if her heart was broken a thousand times over, at least she'd be able to feel the pain. At least she'd know inside herself that she had tried to find happiness, that she hadn't given up on it and let her spirit wither and die.

Beth turned back to the window with a new sense of hope and resolve that seemed to set her soul free at last. A streak of blue flashed through the trees that lined the road below. In seconds Jack's truck was once again parked in front of her house. The ruthless slamming of the cab door and his aggressive strides to the front porch told her he was still angry and upset, but they did nothing to quell the excitement she felt at seeing him.

Her heart beat like a bass drum in her ears. She interlaced her fingers and clasped them tightly together when her hands began to tremble. She felt weak in the knees, but there wasn't much she could do about that at the moment. She wanted to be standing for whatever was about to happen. Her breath caught and held in her throat when she heard the front door close with a boom. She almost choked trying to swallow her trepidation and fear. There were rapid, heavy footsteps on the stairs. And then Jack stood in the doorway.

He didn't look angry or menacing in any way. But there was certainly a resoluteness in the way he was standing that led Beth to believe that nothing short of a S.W.A.T. team could stop him. He held his ground for several minutes while he caught his breath and studied Beth with keen, intuitive eyes.

He stepped into the room and without a backward glance closed the door behind him. Slowly, step after deliberate step, he came toward her. "I was halfway to town before I remembered why I'd been looking forward to seeing you again today. I've thought about it all week. I dreamed about it at night." Beth stepped away as he came within touching distance of her. The glint in his eyes foretold his intentions, and she trembled as a wild burst of energy shot through her. Jack moved closer. "You have the sweetest mouth I've ever tasted, Beth."

Her last step brought her flat against the wall. Jack loomed above her. Her head tilted upward as she stared, trancelike, into his face, unable to utter an objection. Her mind was a jumble of thoughts. She was torn between letting out a scream or a whimper. She jumped when she felt his fingers like feathers around her neck.

Jack shook his head. "Don't be afraid of me, Beth. I wouldn't ever hurt you," he murmured, his hands sliding up her throat to cup her face, his mouth lowering to hers.

The kiss that she was expecting to be hard and possessive was soft, gentle, and tentative, leaving the ultimate choice up to her. It surprised her and gave what resistance she had left time to shatter and crumble into nothingness. Jack apparently could see that she was defenseless. His features softened visibly, growing tender and passionate and full of awareness. He knew her anxieties and understood her fears. His next kiss was aimed at overriding them all.

He pulled her closer before he cradled her in his arms. His body begged to be trusted, and hers was acquiescent. She moved into his embrace willingly, allowed her body to conform to the lean, taut surface of his. Her senses reeled. Her consciousness focused itself in the tips of her fingers and in the streams of excitement that Jack generated with his hands and mouth. She became a sea of desire and need and passion. Each kiss and every touch rippled through her like a tidal wave, washing away layer after layer of painful memory, sweeping away carefully built defenses and years of inhibitions until there was nothing but Jack and the way he made her feel.

Slowly, reluctantly, Jack tapered their ardor until they stood together, breathless and dazed. Beth was aware that he was watching her but made no effort—was unable to make an attempt—to hide the emotions he had aroused in her. A soft, incredulous laugh escaped him. "You see how special this is? And we've just started."

"Jack." Beth wanted to deny his comment, not because she didn't agree with him, but because it was an instinctive response. Denial was a habit, a habit formed to protect herself. And protecting herself was a habit she found hard to break.

Jack placed his finger against her lips and lowered his head again, so that all she could see was the truth of his words in his eyes. "Trust me, Beth. This is something neither one of us has ever experienced before. It's new and clean and fresh. Best of all, it's ours, ours alone. It won't hurt you, I promise. Unless you don't give it a chance to grow. If you try to kill it, it'll eat you up from the inside out, and then we'll both suffer. Trust me on this. Give us a chance."

Something inside Beth wanted to scream and run away. Jack couldn't have been more frightening if he were holding a loaded gun to her head. She began to tremble. She lowered her gaze from his when her vision blurred with tears. There wasn't a thought in her mind of how to respond to him. But in her heart a hundred profound impressions vied to get out.

Jack curled a finger under her chin and lifted her face back to his. In a voice that was nearly a whisper he said, "I won't tell you that I wouldn't ever intentionally hurt you. You'll have to find that out for yourself. And I don't expect you to make any decisions on what I've just said. I'll prove to you that you can trust me, that I'm no one you've ever known before. You'll come around. And when you do, I'll be there."

He placed a gentle promissory kiss on her lips and left before Beth could think of something to say to keep him with her. She stared at the door, conscious only of her breathing. In and out. In and out. Numb, she turned to the window and watched Jack drive away again. This time there had been no anger in his stride. This time he'd walked with confidence, as if he felt a sense of rightness with the world.

Beth wanted to feel that rightness too. She wanted to believe him. She wanted to trust, not only in Jack, but in what she felt inside. Everything he spoke of was there—the desire, the passion, the need. While Beth had stood sentry over her heart in the face of his obvious frontal assault, Jack had outflanked her and silently crawled through the cracks in her defense shield. Slowly and persistently, he had invaded her thoughts and emotions. He'd planted booby traps and sabotaged her efforts to resist him. All that was left was to declare defeat. Beth had lost, and now she knew it.

She wanted Jack. She was falling in love with him, and there didn't seem to be anything she could do about it. She pressed her forehead against the cool windowpane, sighed her resignation, and smiled at the giggly, effervescent feeling that bubbled up inside her. Okay, okay, she thought. He'd done it. He'd gotten to her. And she didn't even mind admitting that she was glad he had. But that didn't mean she was going to go bouncing into this relationship with the innocence of a puppy. She'd been around this block before. This time she knew where she was going and what she wanted. This time she'd be as sure as she could be that it would last forever. If Jack wanted to prove himself, she'd let him. She'd take her time. She'd test him. This time she'd be sure.

Beth was suddenly aware of the silence that surrounded her. It wasn't a trick of her mind either. There was no music, no children's voices—no nothing. When had the music been turned off? Where were the children? These questions raced through her mind as she rushed down the steps to the front room. The evidence that the house had been full of young people was scattered all over the room, but there was no sign of life.

The cans of paint Boodle had been using in the kitchen were neatly sealed and cleaned and waiting for another day. The back door had been left ajar. Without a coat she followed the sounds of chatter and laughter.

"Hey," she called, catching sight of the pack as they walked up the road together, heading for the McKenzie place. "Where do you think you're going?" Scotty broke loose and ran back to greet her. The others looked at her and then at one another, confused and concerned. "What's the matter? What's wrong? Why are you going home?" she asked.

"Did my dad leave already?" Chelsea asked with a frown.

"Yes. Why? Did you need to speak with him?"

"Well, no. Not exactly. I just thought . . ." The girl's voice trailed off uncomfortably.

There was an odd, tense silence. Even the younger children looked uneasy.

"What? What is it?" Beth was getting worried.

They glanced around at one another again. It was Boodle who finally spoke. "When, ah, Mr. Reardan came back, he looked pretty mad about something. But then . . . well, there wasn't a fight, so we"—he looked at Chelsea—"thought maybe we'd take the kids and Scotty to our house for a while, so the two of you could be alone."

"Alone?" Things began to click in Beth's head. It was her turn to feel self-conscious and awkward. "Why would you think that? Mr. Reardan wasn't angry at all. He simply forgot to tell me something . . . and came back."

Beth could tell by the expressions on their faces that she wasn't fooling anyone. Still, there seemed to be some sort of unwritten rule in the back of her mind that prevented her from discussing what actually happened as honestly and as truthfully as she knew she should. Ignoring the incident altogether seemed the best alternative at the moment.

"Come on, I'm freezing out here. Let's go back and fix some lunch. It'll be nap time soon, and then your folks'll be home. And we still have a lot to do." Beth turned and started back to the house, assuming they'd follow. She heard several giggles and an outright laugh. But when she turned to share in the joke, she found Boodle clearing his throat with his hand over his mouth, Chelsea looking over her shoulder at nothing in particular, and the other children smiling happily as they walked along behind her. She smiled back at them, glad that no further explanations seemed to be needed.

Several hours later, with Scotty's room finished, the kitchen half done, and a long-awaited bath in the works, Beth admired the fortitude the kids had displayed during the remainder of the afternoon.

Not once in all that time did one of them mention the fact that the seat of her pants, the back of her sweater, and some of her hair was covered with orange paint, giving the distinct impression that she'd been backed up against a wall sometime during Mr. Reardan's visit.

Seven

Don't hang up.

"Beth?" Jack sounded surprised and confused at hearing her voice on the other end of the line. "Is anything wrong?"

"No. I couldn't sleep," she said, hoping he'd hear in her voice the courage it had taken to call him and not give her a bad time about it. She wasn't prepared to explain why she was making this first step in his direction. She knew only that she had to do it. It was her way of raising the white flag. "I . . . I thought maybe you'd be a little restless tonight too."

There was a slight hesitation before he spoke. "As a matter of fact, I am. I'm glad you called."

"I thought maybe you'd like to talk awhile."

"About what?"

Beth took a deep breath. "Oh, I don't know. I thought maybe since we talked about you last week, we could talk about me this week."

"Sounds good to me."

"Is there . . . anything special you'd like to know?" She wasn't very keen on the idea of getting too personal too soon, but she felt obligated to be as open about her life as he had been about his. She'd made that decision when she'd picked up the phone. This was a new start for her, and she wanted to do it right.

"I have the feeling I'm going to think everything about you is special, so why don't you pick a place and start talking. If I have any questions along the way, I'll just jump in."

Beth smiled. He'd almost repeated verbatim what he'd said to her during their first telephone conversation. Only this time he'd be the one to listen. He wasn't going to push her, she realized, and the anxiety she'd felt eased considerably. He was going to let her come to him at her own pace, and she would be eternally grateful for his kindness and understanding.

She started with her most recent past, since it was the happiest and easiest to talk about. From the time Scotty had been born to her move into the old McKenzie house had been the best as well as the most painful years of her life. She talked about the good times, avoiding little incidental facts such as her husband's rejection and their divorce and how she'd had to live with her mother's pious attitude. Actually, when she set her mind to it, she found a multitude of good things to talk about. It amazed her that there were so many. For so long she'd been dwelling on the worst times of her life and had blocked out the fact that the majority of her life had been fairly normal and very good. Along with the crosses she'd had to bear, she'd had many, many blessings.

"We'd have won that race"—Beth yawned loudly—"if

our river raft hadn't sprung a leak. But how were we supposed to know that Forever Bond glue wouldn't hold that many rubber trash cans together?"

"Common sense?"

"Ha. That would have made things too easy back then. Did you always listen to your good judgment when you were that age?"

"If I had, my life would be totally different now." He didn't sound particularly regretful about the way his life had turned out, merely thoughtful over the alternatives. Beth knew exactly what he was thinking. What would their lives have been like if they hadn't gotten married so young? Would it have been worth not knowing Chelsea or Scott? Had the decisions they'd made as very young adults been worth the pain of their disappointments or had they been meant to be? If they had the chance to do it all over again, would they?

The wire crackled between them as both became introspective. It was Jack who spoke first. "You'll be at the last game Friday, won't you?"

"Yes, of course. I promised to drive some of the girls over to the Do Drop Inn after the game for pizza."

"Could I go with you?" Jack's tone was low and guarded, as if he knew he was pushing his luck and was half afraid of her answer. But Beth had already considered the risks of going public with their relationship.

If they saw each other quietly and discreetly, it would be less complicated and certainly less humiliating in the end, if things didn't work out between them. But visions of them skulking around in the dark and meeting in out of the way places didn't sit well with her. She had a feeling Jack wouldn't be too happy about it either. If they were going to do this, she reiterated to herself, they were going to do it right.

"Yes. I'd like that," she said, not caring if she sounded a little too excited about the idea.

"What do you think? Do you suppose anyone's noticed we're together tonight?" Jack asked.

For nearly an hour and a half after they'd finished their pizza, Beth and Jack had been deep in conversation—real dialogue this time. They were truly communicating with each other. They shared likes and dislikes, views, and theories. Jack teased Beth and made her laugh easily and naturally. Beth couldn't remember the last time she'd enjoyed being with someone as much as she enjoyed being with Jack.

But their communicating didn't stop on a verbal level. From the moment they'd met on the bleachers at the football field, there had been an undercurrent, a tension, a different sort of awareness surrounding everything they said or did. It was present in Jack's glances and in Beth's every touch, casual or otherwise. It filled the air when they smiled and blocked out the world when their voices were low and serious.

It wasn't until a brief pause in the conversation arose, and they scanned the room to get their bearings that they realized they had become the center of attention. Their absorption in each other was bound to stir people's curiosity, but Beth felt as if she were suddenly being viewed on big-screen TV. Jack, on the other hand, seemed prepared for the bold winks and knowing smiles. It didn't appear to bother him a bit.

"Nah," she replied in a waggish way, even as she squirmed in her seat. She felt like a bug under a microscope. "They're probably staring at Scotty. He's not usually this well behaved."

They both looked over at the two-year-old, who after enjoying a late night out past his bedtime, in the cold mountain air, amid a crowd of tolerant and adoring fans at the football game, had succumbed and fallen fast asleep *on* his pizza.

"It's comforting to know that he does sleep," Jack said. The relief in his voice drew Beth's gaze, but all she saw was a soft, warm expression in his eyes as he watched Scotty sleep. Jack turned his head and their gazes met. "I was beginning to wonder when I'd be able to be alone with his mom."

There was no missing the desire in his eyes or the way his lips curled upward in anticipation. Beth felt herself blushing. She knew exactly what he was thinking, what he was looking forward to. It was as if he were reading her heart's list of wishes out loud.

"I like the way you blush. But if you don't stop, they're going to think I'm talking dirty to you." He motioned with his head in the general direction of the people around them while he teased her with his grin. Beth's face grew warm, at the very idea of what he was suggesting, and Jack laughed out loud. "Next thing you know they'll be scooting their chairs up to our table to hear what I'm saying to you."

Beth groaned, covered her face with her hands, and laughed. It was silly to feel giddy and self-conscious and teenagerish. But that's exactly how she felt. A few short weeks earlier she'd felt as old as the mountains. At this moment she felt new, young, and hopeful. She uncovered her face and smiled at Jack. "Just think what they'd do if they knew that talking dirty wasn't all I had in mind for you," he speculated in a voice as gentle as spring rain.

Beth held his gaze long enough to let him know his thoughts didn't frighten her, then she looked away. Making love with Jack, feeling his body pressed close to hers, tasting his kisses, drowning in his touch, had been tempting from the moment she first laid eyes on him. But she wanted more from Jack. Maybe more than she had a right to ask of him, more than he was willing to give. She needed from Jack what she hadn't gotten from the men in her past. She wouldn't deny that he already owned a large piece of her heart, but she couldn't give it all to him until she was sure she could trust him with it. Too much depended on that trust. Her gaze traveled to the sleeping child in the high chair. It wasn't only her happiness she was risking, it was Scotty's as well.

"We'd better get him home," Jack said. When he glanced back at Beth, her sixth sense told her that he'd been reading her thoughts again. He looked ready, willing, and confident to meet her challenge. His broad smile told her he understood her doubts but that in the end he'd prove her wrong.

"I wonder how many of my girls need a ride home," Beth pondered aloud, relieved to be able to put her more serious concerns on a back burner for a while.

The small restaurant was still bustling with activity. But after making a few inquiries, Beth found that the girls that had come with her now had other means of getting home. Jack was very pleased. Unabashed, he offered to follow Beth home. "Now that you're finally seeing things my way, I want to make sure you get there safe and sound."

"And that's the only reason you're going so far out

of your way?" Beth asked him, her expression dubious. Jack was as transparent to her as she was to him. She bent to carefully remove Scott from the chair without waking him up.

"That and the fact that this *is* our first date, such as it was. Tell me what you'd think of a guy who didn't even bother to see his date safely home?"

"I'd think he wasn't angling for a nightcap or—" Her words came to an abrupt halt and another warm, excited flush spread to her cheeks.

"Or what?" Jack coaxed her, grinning. "Let me take him. It's raining," he said. He took Scott gently and easily into his arms. He wrapped the boy's little coat tightly around him, then cast a daring glance at the child's mother and repeated, "Or what?"

"Or a good-night kiss," she said, boldly calling his bluff.

"Know what I'd think of him?" Jack asked, helping to hold Beth's coat with his free hand while she slipped into it.

"No. What?"

"I'd think he was pretty stupid." He leaned toward her ear and in a voice designed to jangle her nerves and send her heart racing, he murmured, "And I'm not stupid. I want a good-night kiss. And I wouldn't mind hanging my nightcap at your house either—if I wore one, that is."

Beth started for the door and was glad he couldn't see her smile of approval. The man's ego was gigantic. She laughed to herself. It wouldn't do to make things too easy for him.

She said good night to the parents of one of her students as they headed through the door in front of her. When the couple bid her and Jack good night as if it were the most natural thing in the world to see them together, Beth was surprised at how nice it felt.

"Midnight, Chelsea," she heard Jack remind his daughter as they passed a table crowded with teenagers.

Beth turned to study the expressions on the faces she would have to see again on Monday. Most of the teenagers seemed absorbed in their own lives, except two. They simply sat there looking very pleased, indeed.

"Got it, Dad," Chelsea said, smiling.

"Night, Ms. Simms," Boodle said politely, and then tacked on a conspiratorial wink. Beth would have frowned and balked right there if the wink hadn't been followed by an easy, gentle grin that held nothing but goodwill and best wishes for someone he considered his friend.

"Good night," she said, returning his smile before she stepped through the door and out into the drizzling rain. They'd had several inches of snow during the week, and the parking lot looked like an outdoor skating rink.

Gracefulness didn't play a part in her movements as she slid over to her car and opened the rear door so that Jack could slip Scott into his seat. Beth stood watching as he buckled her son in and tested to make sure the latch was secure. He was so tall he had to tilt his broad shoulders to get them through the narrow door opening.

Suddenly she went weak at the vision of all that man being in her bed. The most feminine parts of her grew warm and began to tingle. Her heart played a stop-and-go game that set her nerves on end. Her breath seemed to stick in her throat. She'd seen herself with him a thousand times in her dreams, but she was awake now. And she couldn't remember wanting a man more than she wanted him.

"Jack." She uttered his name unconsciously as the vision played on in her mind.

"Mmm?" He stood and looked down at Beth, waiting for her to speak again. When she didn't, when she simply stood there in the rain, he took a closer look at her and frowned. Then his brow rose. His eyes became a stage filled with light, animation, and awareness. An easy grin spread across his lips. His arm came up to rest on the frame of the rear door as he peered over it at Beth, pleased and intrigued.

But before either of them could do or say anything, a blood-curdling scream echoed through the darkness.

"What the hell?" Jack was the first to react. He was halfway back to the door of the restaurant before Beth could set herself in motion. By the time she reached his side, a small group of people had gathered around him. He was hunched down near the ground, and she had to lean over his shoulder to see what he was doing.

"No. Don't touch it. It hurts. Please. Help me," a young female voice cried out hysterically. She had obviously slipped on the icy pavement on her way out and now sat curled up in a ball with her right ankle held tightly in both hands.

"I'm trying to, Kathy. But you have to let me look at it. I won't hurt you, I promise," Jack said in a firm but not uncaring manner. "Let go now."

Beth watched as Kathy Anderson evaluated Jack's competence and finally, reluctantly, allowed him to look at her leg. The girl's tears dragged a line of mascara all the way to her chin. Her sobs racked her body.

"It's broken, Kathy," Jack said. "I think what we'll do is move you inside and call your folks. They're going to want to get you into Newport to get this taken care of."

"They're not home," she wailed. "My brother's wife had a baby. They went to Boise to see it."

"Were you staying alone this weekend, Kathy?" Beth asked over Jack's shoulder.

The girl nodded and then seemed to remember something. "I was supposed to call my grandmother if I needed anything, but she doesn't drive."

"Well, that's no problem," Beth said calmly. "I can drive you into Newport, and we'll get your grandmother's permission for treatment over the phone."

"Look, if you want to go ahead with Kathy," one of the adults in the crowd said, stepping forward, "I can run out to her grandmother's place and bring her into town. She'll probably want to be there for her."

"Sounds good," Jack said. He looked over his shoulder at Beth and added, "I'll drive. The roads will be a mess if this rain freezes."

"We all don't need to go, Jack. I've driven on icy roads for years. I'll go alone. As her teacher, I feel responsible for her." Beth's words were firm and decisive but not hostile. She could see the concern in his eyes and he'd offered to drive the girl because he cared and not because he didn't think Beth was capable of the task.

"You can take her in my car, then. There's more room. Here we go," he said to the girl as he scooped her up off the pavement and into his arms as if she were a small child.

"But . . ." Beth started to protest, looking back at her own car and a sleeping Scotty.

"Would you like me to go with you, Ms. Simms?" Chelsea asked.

"Actually . . ." Beth was about to ask her to take care of Scotty, when Jack interrupted. He had deposited Kathy in the backseat of his station wagon and was on his way back for Beth.

"That's a good idea, honey. You can keep Ms. Simms company on the way home," he said, handing Beth the keys to his car and helping her across a patch of ice.

"What about Scotty?" Beth finally got out.

"We'll trade kids for the night. You take this big one, and I'll take that little one over there."

"*You're* going to take Scott?" She sounded aghast.

"Sure. Unless you don't trust me to."

"No. It's not that. It's just . . . well, I . . ."

"I took care of Chelsea, and she's none the worse for it."

Beth smiled weakly. He was taking her hesitation personally and misinterpreting it. She did trust him to look after Scott. It wasn't as if he were a complete stranger. She was simply amazed that he'd offered. "No. She isn't. Thank you, Jack. I appreciate it."

Jack had been studying her reaction closely and seemed satisfied that she truly was comfortable with his suggestion. He smiled his approval, and said, "I need your keys, unless that toy runs on batteries."

She gave him her keys, and he walked with her over to his car. When he was sure he wouldn't be overheard, he whispered, "Don't forget where we left off. It was getting very interesting."

Eight

I thought you knew.

"No. I didn't," Beth told Chelsea, surprised and wavering on the edge of furious. They were driving back from Newport. It was late and the winding mountain road was deserted. Beth's nerves were frazzled from the emergency with Kathy and then from having to drive home through the low cloud layer that had settled close to the road, decreasing visibility to about three feet in front of the car. Anything could jump out in front of her, and she wouldn't be able to see it until it was too late. Boy, did she hate driving at night.

And to top it all off, Chelsea had disclosed that her father had volunteered Beth to chaperon a ski outing the next day.

"Well, he said he wasn't sure how you'd feel about it, but that he'd ask you. Maybe he just hasn't had the time," Chelsea said, picking up on the tightness in Beth's voice.

"Maybe," she conceded, giving Jack the benefit of the doubt. She'd given in to her needs and her growing feelings for him, but she hadn't forgotten what it felt like to be taken for granted. She felt strong enough to let herself fall in love again, but she'd never be weak enough to be used again. Beth took a deep breath, trying to calm herself. She was overreacting.

She knew full well that the trip to the hospital, the fog, and the ski trip had nothing to do with the uneasy feelings that were running rampant inside her. They aggravated her discomfort, but they certainly weren't the cause of it. How could she have just handed Scotty over to Jack so easily, she wondered. What kind of a mother was she? She hardly knew the man. Well, she knew him, but how well?

It was easy for her brain to tell her that Jack was a good man, that he'd never hurt Scotty. He was a prominent citizen and well liked. Surely Scotty would be safe with him. But her thoughts had very little tranquilizing power over her heart. In her heart a baby and a grown man were incongruous; they didn't go together. Men knew nothing of children except how to make them. Men ran away from children. They didn't want children, didn't love them. Beth knew from experience. Hadn't Jack said that he'd had his regrets in keeping Chelsea? If his wife hadn't been the first to run away, how long would Jack have stayed with her? Deciding to give Jack her heart was one thing. Giving him her son was something she wasn't quite ready to do yet.

"Our driveway is just up ahead there. See the reflectors?"

Beth slowed the car and turned into Jack's drive only half aware that Chelsea was still with her. It was the first time she'd been to his house. She was as eager to see how he lived as she was to get back to Scotty.

From time to time she could see white fencing on either side of the drive. She strained her eyes to see more, but the fog was too thick. The house was set back at least three or four hundred yards from the road. It seemed like an eternity passed in the darkness before they reached the end of the lane. There, a bright porch light lit the way to the house, which was a long, rambling ranch-type affair from what she could see. The immediate area looked neat and tidy. What registered most clearly about the place was that there didn't seem to be anyone home.

Beth searched the mist-laden structure for a sign of habitation, a light from inside, or, better yet, Jack in the doorway with Scotty bundled up and ready to go home. But there was nothing. "No one's home." She stated the obvious as Chelsea pulled on the car door handle, preparing to get out.

"That's okay. I have a key."

"No. I mean, I thought your father would bring Scotty here." Beth's heart automatically constricted with apprehension. Again she told herself that Jack wasn't a baby-napper or someone she couldn't trust with her son. But emotionally, instinctively, a panic rose up within her.

"Me too," Chelsea said casually, unaware of the thoughts racing through Beth's head. "But maybe he went to your house instead."

That made sense. He had her car and her house keys. That's probably where he went. "Yes, of course. Will you be all right here until he gets back?"

Chelsea laughed. "I'm seventeen. I haven't needed a baby-sitter in a long time, Ms. Simms."

"Of course not," she said, feeling foolish. "I worry too much."

Chelsea cocked her head and studied Beth for a moment before she carefully voiced her thoughts. "You know, Ms. Simms, my dad is a really good man. You can ask anyone who knows him. And . . ." She paused briefly. "I think he likes you. If you're worried about me or something, well, I'm glad he likes you."

Something in Beth wanted to scream. She wanted to find her son. She wanted to make sure he was safe. She didn't need a teenager's approval to see Jack. But Chelsea looked so sincere and so ill at ease discussing the relationship between Beth and her father that Beth couldn't help but smile. "Thank you, Chelsea," she said, and the girl smiled back.

For a person who hated night driving, Beth drove the distance between Jack's house and her own in record time. She hardly noticed the fog. Her instincts to be with her baby were primal, and nothing seemed to calm them.

Seeing her car parked in her own driveway did much to decrease her anxiety, but seeing Scotty was uppermost in her mind. She let herself into the house, paying little attention to the noise she was making until she was startled by a loud "Shh."

Beth peered into her dimly lit living room. The only light came from the television, which was playing the last half of an old John Wayne movie. She closed the door quietly and crept into the room. Jack was stretched out comfortably on her couch, looking for all the world as if everything were familiar and under control.

"You're back sooner than I expected," he said, keeping his voice low and soft. "Everything go okay?"

Beth nodded. "Kathy's grandmother was there before they finished taking the X rays. They had to put Kathy to sleep to reduce her fracture, so Chelsea and I stayed with her until it was over, and then we came home."

"Pretty foggy out?"

It was a natural enough question, Beth supposed, but it had nothing to do with what she really wanted to hear from him. "Yes. How was Scotty?"

"See for yourself," he said, looking down at his side. Beth leaned over and moved closer to find Scotty fast asleep in the crook of Jack's arm with his teddy wedged tightly between them. "By the time we got home, he was wide awake from his nice little nap at the Do Drop. So I gave him a warm bath, and we came back down here to let Johnny Carson put us to sleep."

"Why haven't you put him to bed yet? Has your arm gone numb?"

Jack shrugged and looked down at the warm bundle of little boy at his side. "We were comfortable like this."

Beth didn't think Scott looked particularly comfortable squashed in between Jack and the couch. Then again, he didn't look all that uncomfortable either. She suspected that Jack had kept him up simply because he enjoyed caring for him. How many times had she put off his bedtime for the very same reason.

Jack looked up to see the knowing expression on Beth's face and frowned. "Okay. So I miss this. So sue me."

"Never," she said, looking at him in yet another

new light. This man liked babies and wasn't afraid to admit it. He cared for them and took pleasure in them. She loved Jack even more at that moment. But something nagged at her. Scott wasn't his baby. Jack had no responsibility toward him. How would he feel, what would he do if Scotty became sick or naughty enough to get on his nerves? Would he walk away? "I'll put him to bed," she said, throwing her coat over the chair and bending to reach for her son.

"Why don't I carry him and you run up and turn down his bed," Jack said as if he'd been putting Scotty to bed for years. All the way up the stairs Beth tried to shake the sense of rightness that accompanied the domestic scene. It was a queer feeling even to pretend they looked like a normal family. She'd never shared her parenting duties with a man. Three was an odd number, a number she'd never had to deal with before.

"He's almost outgrown his crib," Jack whispered over her shoulder while she tucked the edge of the quilt up around the baby's shoulders. Beth only nodded. She knew Scott was too big for the crib, but he hadn't learned to climb out of it yet, and she hadn't had the extra money to buy a regular bed, not with the cost of repairs on the house.

"He hasn't complained about it," she answered, more hurt than offended. She didn't need anyone to point out her failures to her. She was very aware that she couldn't afford to give her son everything she wanted to give him. She sidestepped Jack and went back downstairs. She could hear him following and knew that he was watching her.

In the living room she turned to face him. He stood in the entryway with his hands in his pockets, his feet braced, staring at her. "Tired?" he asked in a soft, gentle voice that held no other emotion but concern.

If she said yes, she was certain he'd be polite and leave. But when she asked herself if that's what she wanted, the reply was a resounding no. She was hurt and angry over the remark about the crib, but she was also in awe of his way with children. She felt a little guilty for not having trusted him with Scotty, but she was also grateful that he'd taken such good care of him. She didn't want him charging into her life with critical remarks and unannounced plans for ski trips, but she *did* want him in her life. Everything was so new and so confusing between them, she needed some time simply to get used to the idea of having him around. She felt torn between the ever-increasing feelings he aroused in her and the painful recollections of a past he had nothing to do with.

"Not really," she said self-consciously, knowing what the reply suggested. "More keyed up than tired. Do you think . . . would you like some hot chocolate or something?"

Jack seemed to relax. A warm glow came into his eyes, and he smiled. "Hot chocolate, huh?" He paused as if to give it some consideration. "With marshmallows?"

Beth grinned. "Of course."

"Need any help?"

"No. I'll be right back." She started to walk past him on her way to the kitchen, when an electrical tempest seemed to rise up between them. Her eyes met his, and her breath caught in her throat. It was almost as if a force field of magnetic energy developed every time she came within six feet of him. Her heart began to flutter uneasily. "What about cookies?" she asked, hoping to break his spell over her.

"What about cookies?" His voice was a soft monotone.

"Do you want some? They're oatmeal."

"With raisins?" he asked. Then he smiled as if he'd come to some sort of conclusion. A conclusion he was happy about.

"I can't remember."

Jack laughed. "Cookies and hot chocolate sound great." He broke eye contact and walked into the living room. Beth blew out the air she'd been holding in her lungs in a slow, upward direction that ruffled her bangs, and walked back to the kitchen.

She spent most of her time in the kitchen trying to calm her turbulent emotions. She wanted to take things slowly with Jack. If it didn't work out between them, she didn't want to have too much to regret. The trouble was, she could hardly keep her hands off him. His kisses were too fresh in her memory. The feel of his arms was permanently implanted there as well. If she couldn't stay relaxed and keep herself under control . . . well, she'd just have to, she decided firmly, picking up the plate of cookies in one hand and both cups of cocoa carefully in the other.

The television was off and so were most of the lights in the room when she joined Jack. There was a fire coming to life in the fireplace, which worried her almost immediately. She hadn't cleaned out the chimney yet. But of more concern than the flue nests that were bound to catch fire was the matter of Jack. He was sprawled contentedly across her couch again. His shoes were off, and he looked as if he were ready and waiting for her. Which he had been, she qualified, trying to neutralize her anxiety.

"This isn't a very sophisticated nightcap, I'm afraid. Are you sure you wouldn't rather have coffee or a drink?" She would have loved another excuse to go back and hide in the kitchen.

"This is fine," he said. Gingerly taking his cup from her hand, he watched her back off to sit in a chair across the room. "Us old folks don't drink much coffee after midnight—when we're up after midnight. And I'm already a little intoxicated."

"Old," she scoffed, deciding to forget his last remark and the imminent flue fire for now. The first would be too difficult to deal with, and the second might prove to be a much-needed distraction later on, she reasoned. "I wish you'd stop that. Aren't you ever going to let me live that down?"

"Listen, when someone says that the lead singer of the Supremes sounds an awful lot like Diana Ross, you begin to wonder where generation gaps begin and end."

"I know who the Supremes were. I'd just never heard that song before." She smiled, remembering the dramatic reaction she'd gotten from Jack with that small error.

"Yeah. Right. I'll bet you don't even know which Mouseketeer was Cubby."

"The little drummer," she exclaimed victoriously, grateful for the few reruns she'd watched on cable TV.

Jack's brow rose. He was obviously impressed. "The Indian princess on *Howdy Doody?*"

"Summerfallwinterspring. Or was it Winterspring-summerfall?"

"I don't remember, but you're close enough." His eyes narrowed cunningly. "Who won the sixty-eight World Series?"

Beth sank back in her chair, defeated. "I don't follow sports."

Jack sat up with a start, slapping his forehead forgetfully. "Chelsea's going to skin me alive. I forgot to ask you if you'd like to chaperon a skiing expedition to Schweitzer Basin tomorrow. There are only eight kids going. Basically, we'd just be an extra set of wheels going up the mountain. I don't think they could get everyone into one car, so they asked me to chaperon instead of just asking for my car."

Beth felt relieved. He *had* simply forgotten to ask her. "I don't ski," she said, more than a little disappointed that she'd never learned. "And what about Scotty? I impose on the McKenzies all week long. I'd really hate to leave him on weekends too."

"Well, if we were going to spend the night, I'd suggest we take him along. But there won't be any place for him to rest if we don't rent rooms. And I did bring this point up with my daughter, who, when she wants something, can come up with all sorts of solutions for a problem. She called her grandmother to see if she'd be willing to keep Scotty for the day if you decided to go."

"Your mother?"

"A charming woman who, and I quote, 'would love to get ahold of that child and just love him to death.' " His imitation of his mother was very good, but his facial expressions were even better.

Beth laughed. "Are you sure she wouldn't mind?"

"She'd love it. In fact, if I haven't missed my guess here, I'd have to say this whole chaperon thing reeks of a setup. I thought I should warn you."

"A setup?"

"It is my daughter's and my mother's sole purpose in life to see me happily married. And, I believe, you are to be their victim."

"Me?" Beth experienced her first physical hot flash, going from hot to cold and back again in the wink of an eye. She automatically stood, thinking she was too close to the fire. But when moving to the center of the room didn't help, she just stood there not knowing what to do or say next.

Jack laughed. "Relax. As long as we know what they're doing, they can't really control anything, can they?"

"No," she said with a half laugh.

Jack studied her for a few brief moments, then leaned back into the couch. "Come here, Beth." When she hesitated, he cocked his head and said, "It's too late to back out now. You've already decided to give this thing between us a try. You're going to have to get used to sitting next to me sometimes." He patted the cushion next to him, his green eyes challenging her. "Come on."

Beth approached the couch but couldn't seem to remember how to sit. He took her hand and gently pulled her into the crook of his arm. She made a thorough study of her fingernails before she felt his fingers on her chin, drawing her attention to him.

"Let me guess what you're thinking," he said, his face mere inches from hers, his eyes probing. If he guessed her true thoughts, her plan to go slowly was lost. "You're thinking we're moving too fast, that I'm going to jump in and take over your life, start telling you what to do and how to do it. Right?"

His evaluation was too accurate. She lowered her gaze from his to keep him from seeing what else she felt. It was disconcerting, the way he could read her so well.

"Well, you really don't need to worry about it, honey. I admit I was overly aggressive in the beginning, but

I had to do something to get through to you. But now that we've got a program, we can slow down and enjoy it more. I know you're still a little leery, and that's okay. Nothing's going to happen until we're both ready for it. I promise."

Jack made it sound so simple and easy to put one's emotions on a back burner while your mind did an analytical check on a relationship. Was it that easy for him? Heaven help her, Beth was finding it hard to recall her own name. Cool reasoning was out of the question.

"You're being very patient with me," she said, her voice tight with a yearning she found hard to fight.

"I can afford to be. I've already got what I want." When she questioned him with her expression, wondering what it was he'd gotten, he told her. "I don't want to run your life, Beth. I just want to be a part of it. I don't need to rush you, although Lord knows I'd like to. But I don't *need* to, because I know it'll happen. And when it does, it'll be so much better if you haven't got any doubts."

"Who are you?" she asked, incredulous. "I've never met a man as unselfish as you are."

"Ha. Don't you believe it. I'm a very selfish man. I want you, and I plan to have you. But if I come on like gangbusters, you won't be able to heal yourself and then there will always be suspicion and distrust between us. I don't want anything like that lurking just below the surface of everything we do or say. I want you to trust me. I won't even kiss you unless you feel good about it, unless you really want me to. Like now," he said, his deep gaze missing nothing. But he made no attempt to comply with the plea he saw in her eyes. True to his word, he was waiting and letting Beth call all the shots, letting her make the first move.

She was ready to make it. She had no reason to believe what he said. Everyone had good intentions when they first started a relationship. People always meant to do well, tried not to push, always wanted to give their loved one enough space to grow and be themselves. But it didn't always work. Still, Jack's promise meant something to her. She liked the way he kept things so simple. His patience for her trust. He wasn't promising her the moon and the stars and happily ever after. He was giving her time.

She could feel herself relaxing in his arms as she studied the face that had become so special to her. His wise, intelligent eyes, the determination in the set of his jaw, the pain and happiness in the lines around his mouth, and the sensuality of his lips. When exactly had his face come to mean so much to her?

She placed the palm of her hand along the contours of his cheek and felt the heat and vitality of him. "You are a very special man, Jack Reardan," she said, whispering her thoughts aloud.

"I want you to think so, Beth Simms," he returned in a similar tone. He picked up a lock of her blond hair that lay across the front of his shirt and played with it between two fingers. "Does my family's manipulating bother you?"

Beth's smile was gentle and secretive. "No," she said. Her racing heart was getting tired and started to ache for the relief of fulfillment. It wanted the tension to end and demanded satisfaction. She felt Jack's arms tighten a little. She was warm and secure and more content than she'd been in years. All because of Jack.

In a very deliberate manner her fingers slid into the waves of his sandy brown hair, relishing its thickness until they reached the back of his head. She slowly pulled his face closer to hers. Their lips met gently. Beth's eyes closed. Strength and resolve built up within her. She wanted Jack. Her body needed him. Her soul yearned to possess and be possessed. Her second kiss was deeper, giving Jack permission to release his control and become a co-aggressor. His arms pulled her closer. His body grew tense with his desire.

Beth's ardor intensified to the point where she didn't recognize her own actions. It was as if someone else had taken over her body. It was someone else who boldly and unapologetically took what she wanted. She didn't falter or hesitate when her hands reached out to touch and explore Jack's body. She was quaking but not with timidity. Excitement and passion shook her from within. Her world became an inferno of need.

Her next rational action was to look up at Jack. She saw the same fire that raged deep inside her burning in his eyes. They had somehow reversed positions on the couch, with Jack holding her tightly beneath him. She could feel the strength of him pressed hard against her thigh. His breath came in short, rapid puffs across her cheek. His heart beat in cadence with her own. He smiled weakly. It was a smile of wonder and awe.

His grin grew stronger, along with his confidence as he realized in his mind as well as in his heart that she had not only met him halfway but had been willing to take the entire journey with him. "Isn't this great?" he asked, marveling at the experience like a kid on a new adventure. "I knew it would be like this. I knew. I wanted you so badly, and I was so afraid to touch you. I thought you'd disappear.

I thought my mind had conjured you up because I'd dreamt about you so often. I believed that if I touched you, I'd find out you weren't real."

"You didn't act as if you were afraid to touch me," she teased, her voice deep with passion.

He gave her a quick kiss on the tip of her nose and looked as if he were about to get back to some heavy-duty lovemaking, when he suddenly cocked his head to one side and asked, "Are you okay with the idea of my mother taking care of Scott on Saturday? I can vouch for her abilities, but I don't want to push you into anything you're not comfortable with."

"No, that's fine, if she doesn't really mind. I don't know what good I'll be on a ski trip, though, when I don't even know how to ski," she said, skeptical.

"Well, for one thing, you'll be good to look at." He grinned and then placed a sweet, gentle kiss on her lips. "And for another thing, teaching you to ski will give me something to do when everyone takes off, never to be heard from or seen again until they run out of money or need a ride home."

Beth laughed. "You're not really planning to try to teach me how to ski, are you?"

"You bet your . . ." He glanced down at the open collar of her blouse. Beth's gaze followed his as his fingers deftly dislodged the first button they'd come to. ". . . buttons, I'm going to teach you to ski. You'll love it."

"I don't know, Jack. I'm not really the athletic type."

"You won't be able to stop yourself." He eased the two front panels of her blouse aside and looked down at the lace-framed curves of her breasts. His head bent forward, and Beth felt his hot, searing lips press against the sensitive flesh he'd discovered. "You'll see how much fun the rest of us are having, and you won't want to miss out on it."

Beth was still dubious and finding it harder and harder to concentrate on skiing. She was breathing too fast. Her heart was pounding too hard. The muscles low in her abdomen were coiled and pulsating with a will of their own. Her whole body seemed to focus and feed on Jack's every touch.

"Well, you can try, I guess. But don't say I didn't warn you," she managed to say, knowing her voice was unsteady.

"It's a date, then?"

Beth nodded and smiled. Jack beamed. It was as if he took her every acquiescence as a major victory. Oddly enough, she felt the same way. Every time she could agree with Jack and feel good about it, she felt as if it were a triumph over the past, another step toward the future.

He traced her bra line with little sipping kisses. "With any luck at all, we'll get snowed in up there," he murmured.

She was about to ask what he planned to do with the other members of their party if his wish came true, when she felt the clasp on the front of her bra give way. She was surprised at the soft moan that escaped her when his hands cupped the full weight of her breasts. She hadn't realized how badly she'd needed to be touched, how lonely she'd been for so long. Jack seemed to know. His caress was slow and satisfying, painstaking in his efforts to feed her desire as well as his own.

His mouth closed around one hard-tipped breast, and a wave of pure ecstasy shuddered through her body so violently, she almost pushed Jack away in fright. Almost. The pleasure was drugging. Her mind reeled in a thousand different directions, her body an endless vacuum of need. She reached out for

Jack, and he was there, driving her mad with passion. He nibbled the vulnerable tissue below her nipples and scattered adoring kisses across her belly.

She was vaguely aware of the soft whiz of a zipper, and then she felt Jack's hand slowly scorch a path toward the burning heat between her legs.

The phone rang.

Jack groaned like a man on the verge of death. Beth was bewildered. Why had everything stopped? What was wrong? Her mind was so foggy. Then she heard the phone ring a second time.

"If that's Chelsea, wondering where I am . . ." Jack's hoarse threat was left ominously unfinished as he sat up and helped Beth to do the same.

Weakly, she got to her feet and walked with trembling limbs to the phone across the room. She was glad her back was to Jack when she saw how her hand shook as she reached for the receiver.

"Thank heaven's you're finally home. I've been calling all night, and I was worried sick," Beth's mother declared without preamble. "Where have you been? And who's been answering your phone?"

"Mother!" was all Beth could say. And even she could hear the mixture of agitation and dismay in her voice. Her fingers automatically went to the buttons of her blouse and began to fasten each one in a hasty, jerking fashion. She secured her slacks and even tucked the tails of her blouse inside her waistband before she spoke again. "I . . . I was out. There was an accident with one of my students after the game tonight, and I had to take her into Newport. I . . . I had a friend staying here with Scotty."

"A friend?" A black cloud of dread and doom settled around Beth's heart at her mother's words. The fear, suspicion, and disapproval they intoned were familiar to Beth. She'd lived with them nearly all her life. The question now was, did she want to go on living with them?

She turned and looked back at Jack. He was still sitting on the couch, watching her closely. A worried, confused expression darkened his handsome features. He'd obviously seen what her hands had done, heard the uncertainty in her voice, and had no idea of what she was dealing with. His mother had probably never made him feel like a witless fool for caring about someone. His mother probably looked for the goodness in others instead of automatically declaring them evil and untrustworthy. His mother probably believed in the love two people could share. Beth's mother didn't.

Just looking at Jack, knowing his gentleness and patience, his strength and forthright character, gave Beth an inner strength. She'd defied her mother before for the sake of love—except her mother had been right that time. But Beth couldn't let herself believe that her mother would always be correct in her assumption that all men were hateful, hurtful creatures to be avoided at all costs. If she gave in to her mother's fears again, she'd become her mother. And Beth felt great pity for the woman.

"Yes, mother. A friend," she said, smiling at Jack reassuringly. "A very good friend."

That was all it took to start the litany for those doomed to love a man. Beth sank into the chair beside the phone and released a long, resigned sigh. She'd made her decision, and she'd have to live with her mother's bitterness. But even that thought couldn't dampen the feeling she was experiencing. It was as if she had snapped the iron bands that were squeezing the life out of her heart. She could feel it beating easily, unhampered in her chest. Free again to grow, to feel, to love.

Beth looked up as Jack stood and started putting on his coat. "Hold on, Mother," she said, covering the mouthpiece with her hand, not waiting to see if her mother was going to hold on or not. "Jack. Don't go," she pleaded. "This won't take long."

Jack grinned. She could see in his expression the pleasure her words gave him, even as he shook his head. "Talk to your mother. Unless I'm mistaken, I think she's been calling to talk to you all night and hanging up because I've been answering. It might be important—"

"It's not," she said quickly.

"It might be. . . ." His voice was an intimate whisper as he bent and kissed her hard and fast on the lips. "And I'm not really going anywhere. We'll get back to this." He kissed her once more, his lips intense and promising and full of tender passion. "Real soon."

Nine

Careful what you wish for.

Beth shook her index finger in Jack's face, an exaggerated frown on her face. "Didn't your mother ever tell you about making wishes you didn't really want to come true?"

"Who said I didn't really want this one to come true? I may not look happy right now," he said, stifling an exhausted yawn with his fist, "but I'm tickled to death that we're snowed in up here."

Beth couldn't control the tiny smirk that fought its way to her lips. "You're right, you don't look it. I guess I'll just have to take your word for it."

"Well, whose idea was it to invite all these damn kids?" He turned an accusing glare on Beth.

"They invited us. Remember?"

"So how come you wouldn't let me lose 'em in the storm while we still had a chance, huh?"

"I agreed to that. I just thought your idea of driving them off the road was going a little too far," she defended herself, unable to contain her laughter any longer.

They'd sent the young people to their rooms, hopefully for the night, and were standing together on the landing that surrounded the second floor of the first hotel they'd come across. Driving in the blinding snow had become impossible. Jack had rented four rooms. One for the three girls, another for the five boys, and the remaining two for Beth and himself. He'd insisted that the teenagers call home and explain the situation to their parents. He called his mother and let Beth have a conversation with Scotty. And then he'd fed them all at a greasy spoon diner across from the motel.

Beth didn't need to wonder why Jack looked completely worn out. She was. If she'd had to compare her first ski lesson with anything, it would have been ten rounds in the ring with Mike Tyson. Muscles she didn't even know she had were revolting in agony over the abuse she'd put them through that day. Plus the previous night had been long, stressful, and overwrought with unsatisfied desire. And it couldn't have been any better for Jack. He'd spent nearly the entire day hauling Beth out of the snow. She could well imagine how poor Jack was feeling at the moment.

They'd taken the lift up the bunny hill five times, and Beth had fallen on an average of twelve times on the way down. Depending on how she'd fallen, Jack stood there, howling with laughter or frowning with concern. Then he'd pulled her to an upright position, retrieved her skis, and held them steady while she latched them back onto her boots.

"Why don't you just give up, Jack?" she'd cried out at one point, her frustration taking the upper hand.

"This is going to kill both of us. And we have children to raise."

"What? Me give up on you? Never," he declared, deliberately falling into the snow beside her. "What if I'd given up on you two months ago? What then?"

Beth could tell by the look in his eyes that the question wasn't rhetorical or meant to be as humorous as he was trying to make it sound. In that moment he looked so vulnerable and unsure of himself, so unlike Jack Reardan, her heart twisted painfully in her chest, and she said the first words that sprang into her head.

"Then I'd be warm and dry and sitting at home correcting English papers. I'd be lonely and unhappy. I'd be hiding from the world and letting my life slip away without meaning. I'd be clinging to Scott, suffocating him with my need to be loved by someone." She pushed a stray lock of light brown hair off his forehead with a wet, mitten-covered hand, then dropped her hand down to his chest. "I'm glad you're not a quitter, Jack."

The sweetest grin she'd ever seen slowly spread across his lips. His green eyes twinkled like Christmas lights.

"I'm glad too," he said softly. His lips touched hers tenderly. They were cold, or were Beth's lips just overly warm from the excitement? It didn't matter. It was a lovely, dream-breeding kiss that deepened into a promise of fulfillment.

"Whoa, Ms. Simms."

"Way to go, Jack!"

"Hey, you guys."

They looked up to see their wards flailing their arms and swinging their skis on the chair lift above them.

"You two makin' snow angels or what?" they heard one of them call out. "Nah. They're making moguls," another decided. Laughter rang through the mountaintops.

Jack and Beth smiled at each other, then turned scowling faces on their audience, trying not to laugh.

"Okay, people," Beth called back. "We do *Romeo and Juliet* next week. If you hot dogs break any bones, you can count on repeating senior English."

There was a chorus of good-natured groaning as the group disappeared into the fog clinging to the top of the mountain. Jack had been right. That had been the first and last time they'd seen the motley group until it was time to head home.

"This *could* kill us," Jack had said, flopping back in the snow, arms stretched out as if he'd been shot. "I'm pooped. If we ever see the lodge again, let's go in and get snockered on hot wine. The kids can drive us home."

He was joking, of course. He took his responsibilities far too seriously to consider the idea. But they set it as an imaginary goal—a reason to get out of the snow, a reason to keep them moving downhill.

"Driving them off the road seemed like the only way I'd get to be alone with you tonight," Jack was saying, breaking into Beth's happy recollections of their day together. "Since you wouldn't let me do that, I'll have to think of some other way to manage it."

He was wearing a wicked little smile that alarmed Beth instantly. "Jack. We can't. What if they catch us?" she asked cautiously. She felt as if their roles had been reversed. She and Jack were the wary teenagers trying to conceal their activities from eight morally conscious adults.

"That's what I have to figure out," he said easily. He bussed her on the lips and bragged, "I'm a very clever guy though. I'll think of something." He paused, then added in a disgruntled tone, "Although, I have to admit, when I made the wish, it included a romantic lodge room, not a cheap hotel. I wanted our first time to be really special. Something memorable."

Beth smiled. "Jack. I don't think it's going to make any difference where we make love the first time. Something like that tends to be memorable no matter where it happens."

"I was hoping you'd say that." He grinned. "I mean, when a guy gets this close to a dream come true, he sort of feels compelled to see it through to the end. And I'm feeling very compelled at the moment." He wagged his eyebrows at her meaningfully.

She laughed but held firm to her doubts. She stepped back to the door of her room and looked wistfully over her shoulder at him. "Well, good luck. Wish come true or not, it looks a little hopeless to me. Kids aren't stupid, you know." She sighed, resigned. "I'll see you in the morning."

Jack shook his head, regretting her lack of faith. "Long before that, sweetheart. And much sooner than you'd believe."

She opened the door and went in, but before she closed the door she stuck her head back out and said, "Jack?"

"Yes," he answered softly.

"Thank you. I had a wonderful day."

"Me too."

The accommodations weren't the best the state of Idaho had to offer, but Beth could attest to the fact that they had an endless supply of hot water. Long after her shower had penetrated the chill in her bones, she'd stood under the pounding spray and let it massage her tired, aching muscles. Her fingers were pruny by the time she got out to dry off. She wrapped herself in a blanket because she had nothing else to wear while she washed her underthings for the next day and waited for her hair to dry enough so she could go to bed. *And* while she waited for Jack.

She shook her head and laughed at herself. Part of her knew the situation was hopelessly complicated with eight teenagers in the next rooms. She was partially resigned to spending another long, yearning night without Jack—if she didn't fall over dead with fatigue first. Still, something inside of her was wide awake and anticipating a visit from him. She'd spent plenty of time with the man to know that when he set his mind to something, it got done. Come hell, high water, or eight teenagers.

Through the thin motel walls she heard peals of muffled laughter from the girls' room next door. Beth smiled. Teenagers led such a strange life. Everything was so intense for them—life, love, the future. And then, sometimes, they were so childlike, it was hard to believe they cared about anything but the pleasure of the moment. She wondered if Jack was listening to the boys on his side of the wall, several doors down. Was he recalling the ultra highs and extreme lows of his own young adulthood? The laughter and the pain?

There was a ratting noise coming from the door that joined Beth's room to the room next door. It startled her until she remembered that she'd already checked it and that it was securely locked on her side. It was most likely another stranded traveler assuring his safety from his side, she decided, pulling back the sheets on her bed. Her body couldn't wait for Jack any longer. It was too tired. If her mind wouldn't give over to sleep tonight, it wouldn't be because of an overabundance of energy.

She was about to discard her nice warm blanket for sheets that she knew would be icy cold when the handle on the connecting door rattled once more. There was a soft knock, and then she heard her name being called. She approached the door with caution.

"Beth? Are you asleep?" It was Jack's voice.

"How would I hear you if I was?" she asked, giggling softly. Only Jack could manage this, she decided. Only Jack.

"Oh, good," she heard him say, and then in a louder whisper he said, "Unlock your side of the door. I've got a surprise for you."

The surprise was almost too tempting, but then so was her next idea.

"It was very nice of you to get a surprise for me, but I don't think I ought to unlock the door," she said, trying to keep the laughter out of her voice.

"Why not?" She could tell he was totally stunned and bewildered.

"Because I don't know who you are."

"Beth. It's me, Jack."

"Jack who?"

"Reardan," he said, realizing the game she was playing.

"Can you prove that?"

"Yes," he said in a slow drawl.

"How? Tell me something only Jack Reardan would know."

"You don't know who the Supremes are."

"Jack Reardan *knows* that I know who the Supremes are. You can't be him."

"Does Jack Reardan know that you have a little egg-shaped mole on your left breast?" She could tell by his voice that he was wearing a smug expression.

"I don't know. Does he?"

"Yes, he does. Now open the door."

She did. And the real Jack Reardan was standing on the other side. They stood smiling at each other for a long minute before Beth gathered her blanket about her and stepped across the threshold. "You amaze me," she said.

"I know."

"I'm serious." She laughed. "Where did all of this come from?" she asked in wonder as she beheld an ordinary motel room that had become an idyllic hideaway. There were at least a dozen lit candles of various sizes and shapes positioned around the room. A bottle of wine and two long-stemmed glasses sat on the dresser under a mottled mirror with a chipped gilt frame. The linen on the bed was turned down invitingly, pillows puffed and wrinkle free.

Surely it was Shangri-la, Beth decided, or as close to it as she ever hoped to get. Jack's efforts touched a place deep in her heart that was so tender and vulnerable it actually caused her pain. Never in her life had anyone gone to so much trouble just to please her.

"I don't suppose you'd believe that it came with my wish to be stranded here with you."

"Not a chance."

"I have it with me at all times in case of an emergency?"

Beth shook her head and didn't even try to hide

her happiness. Jack took his first step away from the door, closing the distance between them in two more strides. He didn't touch her, but he stood close enough so that Beth could smell the clean, soapy fragrance left over from his shower and feel the heat of his body. His eyes were animated but not with his usual good humor. They looked serious and introspective as they stared at her face, gauging her reactions.

"I was talking to the manager's wife and just happened to mention that we were supposed to get married tomorrow and that we'd brought my daughter and a few of her friends up to ski before we left on our month-long honeymoon. I told her you were terribly upset because we weren't going to get back in time for our wedding and that I wished there was something I could do to cheer you up."

"You didn't really tell her that. Did you?" She knew as well as she knew her own name that he had done exactly as he'd said. She was going to laugh, but suddenly she felt Jack's fingers curl around the front of her blanket. He didn't seem to want to take it from her just then, only use it to steer her in the direction he wanted her to go.

"Mrs. White, the manager's wife, just happens to have a soft heart and a very romantic soul," he said, parking her lightly on the edge of the bed. Then, turning his attention to the bottle of wine, he went on. "She insisted I take this room at half price since it was connected to yours. Then she gathered up all these fine, mood-enhancing candles for me and told me I should buy this bottle of wine from the bar next door. She said you wouldn't be able to resist it."

He held out a glass of dark burgundy wine to Beth

and waited for her hand to snake out from under the blanket to take it before sitting down beside her.

"So? What do you think?" he asked when she couldn't think of what to say next. He had a little smirk on his lips and was looking very full of himself. "Are you going to be able to resist this seduction or not?"

Beth took a small sip of her wine and then set the glass back on the dresser. She wanted to show Jack that he had nothing to feel smug about. She wanted this seduction to take place as much as he did, maybe more. And she wanted to do at least half of the seducing. Her free hand went to the middle button on the front of his shirt and slipped it through the hole before she spoke. "What if the girls need something during the night?"

"Then we'll hear them knock on the door in the other room." Jack leaned toward her upturned face and gently touched his lips to hers.

"What about the boys?" Her fingers blindly moved up the column of buttons, releasing each one in turn.

"I told them there'd be random bed checks throughout the night, and if anyone was missing, I'd break his leg, and you'd flunk him in senior English." He kissed her again slowly, tugging on her bottom lip. "And Mrs. White has the night shift." His little kisses along her jaw and below her ear sent tingles into her arms and down her spine. "She said she'd call here if she spotted any escapees."

"What about your room?" Her hands slipped inside the front of his shirt eagerly, to feel his warmth and strength. She heard him draw in a sharp breath when she touched him.

"They'll believe what they see in the morning," he

mumbled against the sensitive skin of her throat. Beth was sure his words had a significant meaning, but the notion to ask what it was didn't linger. It flickered out of her mind with the rest of her intellectual faculties, leaving her to function on sensory input alone.

Jack's roving lips followed the curve of her neck to her shoulder and on to the vital pulse at the base of her throat. He kissed her passionately on the lips again, and she relinquished all control to him. Jack became the center of her universe. Beth moaned and clung to him. He was the only real thing in a world that was rapidly going out of focus.

She leaned back on the bed and he followed. Beth drew him close, and they shared several deep, drugging kisses. His skin under her hands was smooth and warm, taut and sinewy. His passion was enduring, hot, and overpowering. And then his kisses and caresses became lighter, until at last he stopped altogether.

Beth opened her eyes when his hand moved up to push a few strands of her blond hair away from her face. He was breathing in a long, hard rhythm, as if he were having a hard time controlling it. His lively green eyes were dark and clouded with his own emotions, leading Beth to believe he hadn't wanted to stop at all.

"Was the manager's wife right? Are you finding this hard to resist?" At first she thought he was joking, but his expression was grave.

Beth opened her mouth to speak, but nothing came out. She cleared her throat. "I find you very hard to resist," she said in a husky voice and with a tender smile. "Not that I'm resisting that hard, mind you. In fact, I think you'll find I'm a pretty soft touch where you're concerned."

He grinned and gave her a lazy little kiss. "I did notice you got right into the swing of things, but . . . do you think this is wise?"

"What?" Beth was confused. "Are you trying to talk me out of it now?"

"Lord, no. I want you so badly, Beth, that I feel as if I'm going insane sometimes. But I—" He grew solemn once again. "I love you, Beth. And I want you to be as sure about this as I am."

I love you, Beth? Those words echoed the ones she held deep inside her for Jack. But why did they strike terror in her heart, even as they filled it to the point of bursting with joy and happiness. She knew why. They were words she didn't trust. But she trusted Jack. She believed in him and in her feelings for him. She was sure she wanted to be with him, and that's what counted. Not the words.

"I am sure, Jack. I'm more sure about this than I've been about anything else in a long, long time. I want you in my life and in my bed for as long as I can have you."

Jack took a long second to examine her soul through her eyes for any lurking reservations. Seeing none, he smiled in that silly, boyish way of his, kissed her slowly, and said, "You can have me for as long as you like. I'm not going anywhere."

She gazed at him adoringly. With one hand at the back of his head, she pulled him into a kiss that was meant to convey all the faith and tender feelings she had for him, all the yearning and passion built up within her, and all her hopes and dreams for their future.

Their tongues met and mated. Their breath mingled and became one. Their hearts matched in rhythm and beat as a single unit. Their bodies pressed together, yearning for the same release.

Jack buried his face in the blanket, and she felt a barrage of soft, explosive kisses between her breasts. Cool air pricked her skin as he inched the blanket away from her. His mouth found a hardened bud. She drew him closer to her and ached for the nurturing her body was meant to receive as well as give.

He fed her desire, lavishing her with care, skill, and patience. She arched toward him. The heat inside her built to a fever pitch.

Like an infinitely kind and gentle master, he rose up to view all that was his. The blanket no longer shielded her, and he beheld her with such longing and emotion that she began to quake with a need so great, she felt she might split wide open if it wasn't satisfied soon.

"Jack, I want you so much," she said, hardly recognizing her own lust-thickened voice. Her fingers slid inside the top of his jeans and tugged firmly on his belt. His hand covered hers to stop the pull, but he didn't answer her demand.

She came to her knees on the bed, comfortable with her nakedness, and looped her arms around his neck. Instantly, his hands were on her hips, then on her soft, fleshy bottom as he pulled her close to the hard core of his passion. He pressed her breasts tight against muscles carved by hard work. He was rigid with pent-up energy.

"Jack. What's wrong?" she asked softly, concerned.

He closed his eyes in frustration, sighed, and then gave her a little squeeze. When he looked at her again she could see in his eyes that he was worried about something.

"What's wrong?" she repeated.

His hand shook as he placed its palm along the side of her face. He shook his head. "I don't know, Beth. I've made love to you a thousand times in my mind, but I never knew you were this small. I don't want to hurt you. I can feel myself losing control. You're so tiny and frail. . . ." His voice trailed off.

Beth couldn't help it. She laughed out loud. Merrily. Joyfully. "Is that all it is? Oh, Jack, you wonderfully stupid man." This time she caught him off balance and pulled him down on the bed with one easy yank. She straddled his hips with her legs and began to loosen his belt. "You won't hurt me. I'm a little shorter than some women, but I'm tougher than most. My mama didn't give birth to no China dolls, you know," she said, teasing him and an easily excitable muscle low on his abdomen. "Speaking of which, I've even given birth. And you can't expect me to believe that making love with you would be worse than that? Lift up."

He lifted his hips off the bed so she could remove his jeans and briefs. He waited for her to remount him before he spoke, his voice still filled with worry. "That's just it. I don't want you to think it's worse than anything. I want you to think of it as something wonderful, not something painful or uncomfortable. I want to make you happy. I'd die if ever I hurt you."

He ran his hands up and down the sides of her body, and she shivered as cool air and excitement assaulted her senses at once. "And here I was, worried that I might be too much for *you*." She began to plant kisses in the small mat of coarse, dark hair on his chest. "I'll tell you what, Jack. I'll let you know if you hurt me, and you can feel free to do the same. Okay? If driving him mad was the only way to convince him of her strength, that's exactly what she'd do. "Does this hurt?" Jack groaned weakly, and Beth's smile reflected the feeling in her heart.

It didn't take long. An inferno raged within him in seconds. She touched him, stoked the intensity of the blaze. She smiled down into eyes that were glazed with mindless passion. She fell easily beneath him.

He ravished her with his kisses, tortured her breasts to an exquisite pain. His hands conquered every inch of her body and claimed it as his own, for all time. Voraciously, he entered her warm, moist core. With his fingers he discovered the key that unlocked her wildest dreams, excited her to delirium. She gave herself up to him without fear or doubt. Together, in a frantic, frenzied state of ecstasy, they passed over the edge of reality.

Already she could feel him pulling away. Their skin was still damp and they were breathing hard, and she could feel him easing his weight off her chest and pelvis. With effort her arms locked around his waist and pulled him back to her.

"Don't leave me," she murmured against his shoulder as she breathed in the heady, musky scent of him.

"I won't. I was just trying to take some of the pressure off so you can breathe." His voice was deep and drowsy.

"I can breathe fine."

He lay still for a few minutes, and Beth wallowed in her contentment. "Do you know how it makes me feel when you cover me so completely with your body?" she asked. "I feel warm and safe and protected. And I'm not ready to give that feeling up yet. What can I do to keep you here a little longer?"

Jack rose up on his elbows and looked down into her face with great tenderness. She had to admit it was a little easier to breathe, and she wouldn't have missed that look for anything. She'd never in her life felt so cherished. At that moment there was no doubt, no sense of impending doom in her heart. She felt only a unique sensation of rightness in her mind, her heart, her soul.

"You don't ever have to give it up, Beth. I want you to feel like that all the time. In and out of bed. On top of me, below me, or at my side. I love you." He kissed her sweetly, adoringly, then covered her with his body again.

They lay together, silently rejoicing in their happiness. For every minute they were together, a hundred in Beth's past were washed away. She'd discovered and donned a cloak of golden hope that helped to repel the elements of fear and doubt and bitterness that had been her environment for so long.

There was a soft tapping on the door. Beth heard it, but she snuggled into the warmth that surrounded her and dismissed it from her mind. The tapping came again, a little louder. Jack heard it this time. It startled him from a sound sleep. He was out of bed and had his pants on before Beth could focus her eyes.

She heard him release the chain on the door and saw him peer around it as he opened it just enough to see who was on the other side.

"Oh. Good morning, Mrs., ah, White. Is anything wrong? Have the kids made a break for it?" If Jack's mind was as clear as his voice, it was functioning very well. Beth had forgotten all about their charges. Then again, Jack had a few more years of experience in dealing with Chelsea and her friends.

"No. No. Now, don't worry, Mr. Reardan. I'm off duty and was just going home, and I thought I'd drop by here and let you know that I didn't see hide nor hair of any teenagers last night but . . ."

"Oh, good. And I really appreciate all you did for me last night, Mrs. White. Thank you." Jack rubbed one foot over the other to ward off the cold air blowing in under the door.

"I was glad to help. Did . . . everything go well?"

"Oh, yes, ma'am. Real well. Thank you." Beth could hear the laughter in his voice and would have bet her last penny that he winked at the woman.

"Well, good. I'm glad and I'll be going now, but I just thought you might like to know that I saw your kids heading out toward Murphy's about fifteen minutes ago. They stopped at the desk to ask directions from my husband."

"What's Murphy's, Mrs. White?" he asked quickly, worried again.

"Oh, it's just a little doughnut and coffee place, Mr. Reardan. Don't you worry. They were just scoutin' out some breakfast. They'll be back real soon."

"Thanks, Mrs. White."

The woman left, and Jack closed the door, leaning on it heavily as he turned back to face Beth. "You know, if I'd wanted those damned kids to get up early, they'd have slept till noon," he said with a weary shake of his head and a lopsided smile.

Beth laughed. "What time is it? I don't even remember falling asleep."

"Me either," he said, crawling across her to get to

his watch on the other side of the bed. "Eight-thirty. They probably asked at the desk last night for a wake-up call just to spoil my morning."

"Why? What were you planning to do this morning?" Jack just looked at her. She stared back blankly. He wagged his eyebrows up and down lecherously. "Oh," she said, then she laughed again. It was all she seemed to be able to do. Laughter just seemed to bubble up inside her without reason. Or maybe there was a reason. Maybe it was the happiness that filled her heart when she looked at Jack. Maybe that was it.

"Do you suppose they know about last night?" she asked, strangely unconcerned about anything except the way Jack's hand felt as he brushed her hair away from her face.

"No," he said, kissing her once gently, and not so gently a second time. He groaned and kissed her again before sitting back and looking at her regretfully. "But I think I should run down to Murphy's before they come looking for us."

"I'll go with you. It''ll only take me a couple of minutes to get ready."

"No." He said it so adamantly, he surprised her. "They think I've got this terrific batting average with women. If we go in together, they'll get suspicious."

Beth nodded her understanding, then asked, "And do you?"

"What?" he asked, pulling on his shirt while he looked on the floor for his socks and boots.

"Have a terrific batting average?"

He stopped and looked at her. Was she jealous? Or was she afraid that she might be just another home run? He grinned. "No. I don't. Or at least I didn't until last night. And now I feel as if I've just won the World Series."

She laughed again. "I don't follow sports, remember? Is that good or bad?"

Jack cast her a dubious glance. He finished tying the laces on his boots and walked around the bed to sit beside her. "Winning the World Series is the best." He bussed her on the lips. "And you know it." He tickled her unmercifully.

"Jack. Stop. Oh, please. Stop. Jack. Stop." Her cries brought no relief.

"Tell me you're happy."

"I'm happy."

"Cross your heart and hope to die?"

"Cross my heart and hope to die."

"Stick twenty-five needles in your eye?"

"Yes. Yes. Please, stop."

"Kiss me?"

"Yes." Immediately the tickling stopped, and his mouth closed over hers before she could catch her breath. But that was all right, she shared his.

"Morning, skiers," Jack said cheerfully, his hands deep in the pockets of his ski jacket as he sauntered up to the teenagers' table in Murphy's Donut Hole.

"Morning, Mr. Reardan," all eight voices intoned in disharmony. The semi-angelic faces that stared back at him made Jack a bit uneasy.

"Where's Ms. Simms?" Ralph "Buns" Bunsinger asked, looking for all the world like an innocent.

Jack raised his brows in confusion and looked around the room. "I don't know. The man at the desk said you'd all come down here for breakfast. I assumed she was with you."

"We knocked on her door before we left, but she didn't answer," Patty said.

"Well, maybe she was in the shower," Jack commented.

"We knocked on your door too, Mr. Reardan," said Carl, finding it difficult to look as innocent as Buns.

"I told them what a sound sleeper you are, Dad," Chelsea said, grinning hard and watching some ice melt in her paper cup.

Jack knew the jig was up. "That's my girl, Chels. Stick up for your old dad, and then go out and have a Coke for breakfast."

The seven other knowing smiles were now in plain view. They weren't malicious sneers, just young I-gotcha grins that Jack found hard not to return.

"Okay. Now, listen up," he said in a good-natured tone. "I want this act cleaned up before Ms. Simms gets here. She doesn't need to know that I'm not as clever as I thought I was."

Ten

I love you.

They were familiar words to Beth. Words she'd heard before. Words she'd once believed in. Words she had placed her hopes and dreams in. Words that she'd let control her life. But they were words that meant nothing to her anymore.

Her father had loved her—but not enough to stay with her. And not enough to come back when she needed him. She'd married young because Cal had said he loved her. And she had loved him desperately. They'd moved to Seattle so he could go to medical school, and she worked, sometimes two jobs at once, because they were building a dream together. She'd fought viciously with her mother during those years, refusing to believe the poor, bitter woman's prediction that Cal would leave her with nothing as soon as he finished school.

After his residency Cal promised she could attend college so that she could do something with her own life. But when she became pregnant with Scotty, Cal's love wasn't extended to their baby. Because he'd loved Beth, he'd given her the freedom to choose between him and the baby.

There was never any real choice for her. And there was never any real love between them. In the end she'd returned home to her mother, to relive her life over and over again through her mother's constant, bitter words.

Now there was Jack. Jack said he loved her. And she felt his deep feelings for her in a hundred different ways. He made her happy. He filled her with satisfaction. From moment to moment she basked in his tender emotions. The scars of the past were healing, but the future didn't seem to exist for her, except where Scotty was concerned. With Jack there was only the present—which was more than she had hoped for a few months earlier. She was grateful, but she wanted more.

Deep inside she harbored a monster that fought against dreams of growing old with Jack. It refused to allow her to make plans that involved a time span of longer than two weeks. It controlled all her hopes and kept them at the bare minimum. She was grateful for each day she had with Jack. The doubtful demon kept her on tenterhooks, loving with all her heart and waiting for the bottom to drop out of her world—again.

"We have to talk about it sometime," Jack was saying, his voice rippling her dark pool of thoughts. "Now that I've got you under my spell again, totally naked and vulnerable, it shouldn't be too hard to get the answer I want from you."

She cupped his face with her hands and smiled up into eyes that saw too much of what she was feeling. "Oh, Jack. We've been over and over this. Can't we just enjoy what we have without messing it up with marriage?"

"But I love you. I want to spend the rest of my life with you. I want you to give me a baby before Chelsea makes me a grandpa." He was trying very hard to keep the conversation light and teasing and not make her feel too pressured, but Beth could tell it was costing him.

"Chelsea is going to college and then medical school. That's eight years. Tack on another year for her residency and nine months of gestation, and you still have nearly ten years before she'll make you a grandpa," she reminded him. "Will you relax?"

Her hands smoothed out the muscles that looked like coiled ropes across his shoulders and down his arms. They'd made love so often over the past few months, she felt as if she knew his body by heart. And still their loving was new each time, strengthening the bond between them. It didn't matter what her insecurities whispered to her in the dark when Jack wasn't there, they couldn't stop her from loving him totally.

Jack couldn't be soothed or diverted this time. With his skin still damp from their lovemaking, he left her to sit on the edge of her bed. For long minutes he sat with his back to her as if searching for the words that would make her see his side of things. He could have saved himself the effort; she knew and felt exactly what he was thinking.

Finally, he sighed heavily and turned to face her with a compassionate expression. "I'm sorry, Beth. I'm trying to be patient. I really am. The last time I asked someone to commit to me, it was under du-ress. We both knew it wasn't what we wanted, but I just couldn't bring myself to give away my own child. I begged Chelsea's mother to give the marriage a chance. And she did try. It just wasn't enough for her." He placed one hand on the bed and leaned toward her as he grew more earnest. "I want so much for us, Beth. For you. For me. For Chelsea and Scott. I want us to be a family. Chelsea loves you, and I want to be Scott's dad. I want us to live together in one house and make love whenever we want to, instead of sneaking around the way we have been." He threw his free hand up in agitation. "Hell, we haven't even been fooling anyone. Chelsea . . . well, the whole damn town knows we're sleeping together."

Beth might have taken exception to this under other circumstances. Appeasing a small town's conscience was no reason to get married. But she knew Jack. And she knew what he was about to say. "I'm sick of trying to hide something everyone knows about. I want the whole world to know I love you, and I don't like having to sneak around. I'm proud of what we have together."

His voice had risen with his emotions, and when he caught himself shouting at her, he took a deep, bracing breath and spoke more calmly. "I know I'm asking a lot of you. That creep you were married to used you and then ran out, leaving you holding the bag. I also know after all this time that there's not a damned thing I can do or say to convince you that I'm different. I keep hoping that it's just a matter of time. That you'll eventually figure out that I'm determined to make you understand how much I love you, how much you mean to me. But I don't mind telling you that it's getting damned frustrating." He was shouting again, and the realization seemed to make him even more angry.

He looked away as if the sight of her were painful to him, and Beth ached to ease his mind. Why couldn't she say, "Okay. Okay. I'll take my chances again, let's give it a shot. Let's get married." Why couldn't she just accept that his love was as deep and abiding as he professed it to be? What was she waiting for? A bolt of lightning, a burning bush? Some heavenly sign that whatever Jack said was true? She hated to see him so unhappy, but all she could honestly tell him was "I'm sorry, Jack."

He shook his head as if an apology weren't necessary—or helpful. And when he spoke, his voice was strained with his effort to make everything sound normal between them.

"Do you still want me to stop at Cory's tomorrow after work and help you get Scotty's new bed home?"

"Yes. Please. If it's no trouble for you." Beth was also having trouble stepping from the emotional to the mundane. A very odd feeling prickled the skin on the back of her neck. She hated leaving the small rift between them unmended. And yet, something inside her was eager to see what would happen next.

Would Jack grow weary of waiting for her to make up her mind? Would he finally lose all patience and walk away from her? Would they fight and argue about her weakness and her refusal to commit her heart totally to him until, in the end, Jack threw up his hands in disgust and purged her from his life? Was that what she wanted? Was she testing him? Was she intentionally pushing him to his limit to see what he would do the first time things didn't go entirely his way?

She hadn't acknowledged it before, but that was exactly what she was doing. She couldn't seem to help herself. She had to test and push and torment. She had to know how much Jack would take and how he would react. She had to know.

They agreed to meet at Cory's Furniture Store the next afternoon, and Beth walked him to the door. His single kiss was cooler than usual, but he made a point of telling her he loved her. And while there was a tiny fraction of her that was waiting for him to give up, a much greater part of her was joyful that he had not.

It was nearly one in the morning when he backed his truck out of her driveway. She turned out the porch light and pressed her back against the door to face the empty house.

With Scotty asleep and Jack gone, she was alone. How had she ever been able to convince herself that alone was the best way to spend her life? Thinking of that poor wounded animal that was Beth Simms only a few short months earlier wrenched her heart and made her shudder. Jack had saved her. He'd replenished her spirit, saturated her heart with a new zest for life, and charged her to the max with unqualified happiness. How could she treat him so horribly? How could she deny him, when they both wanted the same thing?

Since the night they'd consummated their love, they had been as one. And except for the fact that they weren't living in the same house and eating breakfasts together, they were a family. The night *Romeo and Juliet* was presented to the public they'd waved Chelsea off to be with her friends and then taken Scotty home to bed. They'd started a ritual of tucking him in together, and ever since that night, those few late hours of the day had been theirs, their time alone.

On Thanksgiving Beth had filled her house with Reardans and on Christmas Mrs. Reardan cried at having another baby celebrate his Christmas in her home. On Valentine's day Chelsea had taken charge of Scott so Beth and Jack could go to Spokane for a romantic night of dinner and dancing. Jack had even volunteered to spend a grueling afternoon with her mother, after which he'd said not a word but had simply held Beth in his arms as if she were the most precious thing he'd ever discovered.

Between holidays their lives had settled into a routine of sharing dinners and having long discussions about their days, the life around them, and life in general.

The more Beth got to know Chelsea, the more she'd come to care for the bright, ambitious young woman and the more she became convinced that the girl had a level head on her shoulders. She wouldn't swear to Jack that Chelsea and Boodle weren't sleeping together, but she felt certain that if they were, Chelsea was taking all the right precautions.

Scotty, who seemed to be learning a dozen new words a day, finally started calling Jack "Yak" but still thought of him as Daddy. Jack could kiss Scotty's boo-boos just as well as Beth, he could throw a ball better, he could teach him how to aim straight in the bathroom, and he was a lot more fun to wrestle with. And to Beth's constant dismay, Scott's behavior was drastically improved in Jack's presence. He seemed to have a healthy respect for Jack's deep masculine voice. She even found that sharing her baby was easier than she ever thought possible. Her joys doubled, her trials were cut by half, and her anxieties were consoled, because she could share them with Jack.

All in all, she had to admit, they had all the makings for a wonderful family. The only thing that stood in their way was her fear of being rejected once again. She could well understand Jack's exasperation—she felt it herself. But the fact remained, she couldn't afford to make another mistake.

"I don't suppose you thought to ask Boodle to meet us at your house to help move this thing up the stairs," Jack said as he covered with a thick blanket the new chest of drawers that matched Scotty's new bed. He tied one end of a rope to the pickup and wound it around the piece of furniture to keep it in place before tying the other end of the rope to the opposite side near the tailgate.

"Well, I hadn't planned on getting the dresser too. And I thought you and I could manage the bed. But the whole set was such a bargain, I didn't think I could pass it up."

"In other words, you didn't call Boodle," Jack said. He hadn't made the slightest effort to conceal his temper since he'd met Beth at the furniture store. He'd been snarling and snapping like a mad dog at everyone they met. She wasn't sure where this uncharacteristic behavior was coming from, but she was beginning to hope that he wasn't planning to spend this particular Friday night at her house. She was trying to be patient but, quite frankly, his attitude was getting on her nerves.

"No. I didn't call Boodle. I didn't think we'd need him."

He turned his back on her to finish securing the

furniture, and she heard him mumble something about her thinking too much and then not thinking at all. She was sure he hadn't meant for her to hear it, and she was positive she didn't want to call him on it while he was in his present frame of mind, so she let it go.

"If you and I can get it into the house, we can leave it downstairs and then move it the next time Boodle comes over. All Scotty really needs now is the bed anyway," she said lightly, offering the best solution she could think of, wondering how she could alleviate the tension between them.

"Fine." His response was dull and flat as he jumped from the flatbed and then slammed the tailgate in place. "You follow. Honk if anything looks loose."

More and more she was beginning to suspect that his black funk was for her benefit, and she had a pretty fair idea what she'd done to cause it. A nervous, panicky churning began in her stomach. Was this the beginning of the end? A dull ache pulsed in her temples. Had Jack reached his limit? He'd hardly looked at her in the past hour. Was it over?

Jack got into his truck and started the engine. He looked back at her through the rearview mirror. His green eyes held no humor. The set of his shoulders showed his irritation. She fumbled with the keys, dropping them on the floor. Jack looked everywhere *except* into the rearview mirror, as if her actions were making him angrier.

He was a half block ahead of her by the time she got her motor in gear. He had to slow down for the flashing light at the intersection to the state highway before heading north, and Beth caught up with him there. They hadn't gotten three hundred yards down the road before Jack suddenly slammed on his brakes and pulled over to the side of the road. Beth followed his lead, perplexed. His door flew open and bounced on its hinges. She opened hers cautiously. When he started across the road with long, purposeful, angry strides, she had to run to catch up with him.

"Jack! What's wrong? What are you doing?" she called out, reaching for and finally grabbing hold of his arm. Her weight made him falter but it didn't impede his progress. He kept charging forward, dragging her along beside him. "Jack. Stop. This is crazy."

"Crazy?" he asked, coming to a dead stop in the middle of the highway and turning on her in anger. "This isn't crazy. Listening to *you* was crazy," he shouted.

Beth frowned at him. Her senses raced, aware that she was in grave danger of being hit, either by Jack or any one of a thousand trucks that traveled the highway on a daily basis. Confused, she stood wondering how she'd gotten herself into such a predicament.

"Look," he said, pointing to a low white stucco building behind a stand of trees some distance up the road. Beth strained her eyes to see something out of the ordinary about the sight. She was beginning to think Jack had X-ray vision or had gone completely off his rocker, when she saw Boodle's unmistakable bright red truck moving along the service road.

She was still frowning, missing Jack's point altogether when she looked at him. Seeing Boodle's truck leaving a community health clinic wasn't much to get excited about.

"Chelsea's with him," Jack said simply, breaking loose of her hold and heading for the clinic.

"Jack, wait," she said, reclaiming his arm just as the truck stopped at the main road. They both watched as the two young people in the truck looked in their direction. Chelsea rolled down her window and waved furiously at them, smiling. Boodle tooted his horn in recognition, and then they drove away—north, toward home.

Jack continued to stand there. He looked drained, weary, even a little older all of a sudden. Beth realized he'd probably been worried that Chelsea might be hurt when he saw Boodle's truck at the clinic. She understood now and wanted to comfort him. "You see. Chelsea's fine," she said cheerfully, pulling him back to the side of the road and out of harm's way. "You had me scared to death for a minute there, Jack."

Jack looked over his shoulder at her, and Beth gasped at the fury that still marred his handsome features.

"Why should you be scared? She's not your daughter. She's just some kid in your English class, right?"

His words pierced her heart like ice picks. His eyes were accusing her. "Jack, no. You know that's not true. I love Chelsea."

"Yeah, right," he said, his tone sarcastic. "Leave them alone, Jack. Chelsea's very mature, Jack. Let's talk to 'em, Jack," he mimicked her words. "Why did I ever listen to you? Hell, the choice you made at eighteen was just as stupid as the one I made. I should have gone with my instincts on this. I should never have let you talk me out of breaking them up."

"Oh, no, Jack. You don't really think Chelsea's pregnant, do you?" It was a possibility, but Beth couldn't bring herself to believe it.

"Well, why the hell else would two teenagers go to

a health clinic alone together? Chelsea doesn't even take aspirin for a headache without telling me. I've made the appointment and paid the bill for every physical examination she's had since the day she was born," he ranted. "Why else would she go to a clinic without telling me?"

"Oh. Well, there's a lot of reasons," Beth stammered, the gears in her brain shifting into overdrive. "Ah . . . maybe she was injured. But . . . but not seriously . . . a little cut or something, and she didn't want to worry you. Or maybe Boodle had a minor injury, and she went with him. Or maybe they just went in for some information for a school project or something. It could be anything. I think you're jumping to conclusions, Jack."

As her words penetrated, the storm in his eyes began to fade away to a clear, thoughtful stare. Beth took hope and went on. "She sure didn't look like an unwed teenager who had just been told she was pregnant, did she?"

"What if she just found out there was a way to get rid of it before anyone else found out about it?"

"Jack," she said, her voice full of scorn. "She wouldn't be happy about that either. And if she were in trouble, you'd be the first person she'd turn to, and you know it."

"I used to know it when she was younger. But she's so damned independent, she could do most anything and I might not hear about it until after the fact."

"Not something like that. She'd tell you."

He didn't look absolutely sure about this, but he was calmer. It was Beth who still had a lot of uneasiness about the situation. Her heart told her she was right. Chelsea's visit to the clinic was perfectly innocent. But in the back of her mind were the memories of all her deceptions when her mother had tried to separate her from Cal. She had smiled sweetly into her mother's face and told her boldly that she was going to meet with her girlfriends but had met Cal on the sly. The night she'd gotten married, she had told her mother she was going to be at a sleepover at a friend's house. Beth, better than most people, knew how devious a person could be when they thought they had no choice.

They took the drawers out of the dresser and had no trouble moving it into the house. Beth thought they could get it up the stairs, too, but Jack still felt it was too much for them to handle. He brought the bed frame, spring, and mattress in, and Beth suggested leaving them downstairs as well, since it was growing abundantly clearer by the minute that he was chomping at the bit to get home and talk to Chelsea. But he insisted on taking them up. "It isn't heavy. I'll put it together tomorrow and take down the crib, if you can wait till then."

Beth could wait forever on the hope of a tomorrow. Whole years of her life had passed while she'd waited for her father to come back. She'd wait longer for Jack if she had to. Waiting was no problem. It was the lack of hope of ever seeing him again that she couldn't bear.

"You know," he said, coming down the stairs, "if Chelsea is in trouble, I can't lay all the blame for it at your door. You offered your opinion, and I took it. If it was poor judgment, it was poor judgment. But I think I've made an even greater mistake in this mess than not listening to my better judgment."

Beth couldn't think of anything he'd done wrong. She'd always thought his rapport with his daughter was wonderful. She'd even envied it in weaker moments. She stood silently waiting for him to confess his error.

"I've been setting a lousy example for her. I might have gotten home at fairly decent hours, but she wasn't fooled for a minute. She's known all along that you and I were sleeping together. And you and I aren't any more married than she and Boodle are. She probably thinks that if it's okay for us to do it, it's okay for her."

The self-contempt in his voice made Beth's skin crawl. Her stomach tied itself into a heavy knot. Her nerve endings began to jump in warning of imminent disaster. "Jack. She doesn't think that way. She knows there's a whole world of difference between our situation and hers." She put a hand on his arm. "If what you're thinking is true, if Chelsea is pregnant, you can't blame yourself. She's a bright, intelligent girl. She knows the risks. She knows we're adults and that she's still young, with so much to do before she gets tied down with a baby. If she decided to make love with Boodle, she would have decided to do it even if you and I had never met."

Jack shook his head, bewildered, listening only to his own inner voice. "I'll never be able to forgive myself if I've let this happen to Chelsea. I've been so wrapped up in my own life, I must have ignored the signs."

The pain he felt was almost tangible. He couldn't look her in the eye, couldn't see the denial of his words in her expression or the guilt he was making her feel. Worst of all, he couldn't know the terror he provoked in her heart. That he regretted all the love they'd shared caused Beth excruciating hurt. Deep inside, Beth had words she wanted to say, words that needed to be said. But they stuck in her throat when she heard his sigh of remorse.

"Second-guessing this whole thing isn't getting me anywhere. I'm going home to talk with her." He gave Beth a hard, steady look as if trying to make up his mind about something. "I was thinking, too, that maybe we could use some time apart. To sort of . . . evaluate our relationship a little. Do a little re-thinking, you know?" he said, opening the front door. "I'll let you know what happens with Chelsea." He pressed a kiss to her forehead, but it seemed more a thoughtless, obligatory act than a show of affection. Something inside her withered and died.

Beth stood numbly in the doorway and watched him drive away without looking back. Her heart constricted into what felt like a hard, heavy rock and sank to the pit of her stomach. Her head began to pound relentlessly, and her muscles quivered. She wiped a stream of tears from her eyes, only vaguely aware that she was crying.

Eleven

Is that all there is?

Beth looked down at Scotty and rattled the empty cracker box at him. "All gone," she told him.

She was out of everything. There were no more crackers, no cookies, no chips or candies. There wasn't any cheese, peanut butter, oatmeal, or raisins. Even the apples and bananas were gone. She was out of everything. Out of food. Out of love. Out of hope.

Scotty looked back at her with innocent bright blue eyes, and the raw, jagged edges of her shattered heart began to bleed anew. it was agonizing to think that he might someday have to feel the way she did at that moment. Why did he have to grow up? Why couldn't he just stay little and unscarred forever?

"How about a scrambled egg?" she asked him lifelessly.

"No."

Beth took two eggs out of the refrigerator. It didn't

seem fair to Beth that the only person in the house with any control over his life should be a two-year-old. And besides, she was out of everything else.

She cooked the eggs, set Scott's breakfast in front of him, and listened with an apathetic ear to the sound effects that accompanied his disgust. At least he had the gumption to fight back, she thought absently. Circumstances had dealt him a dirty blow, leaving only eggs for his breakfast, but he wasn't about to eat them without a protest. Not the way his mother would, she thought derisively.

Then again, he was just two. He was still fresh for the fight. He wasn't a pro like his mother. He hadn't yet taken punch after punch after punch, only to have to stand up and find the courage to take another. Beth felt as if she'd been beaten by a champ this time. Her gaze fell away from Scotty. She looked anywhere but in his direction. He was a living reminder that eventually, she'd have to get up again. And she would. If nothing else, Jack had taught her that.

The world wasn't going to go away and leave her alone. People would continue to creep into her life and wreak havoc in her heart. She couldn't—wouldn't—live the way her mother had. Isolation was just as painful as loving proved to be time after time. In a state of emotional shutdown, there was nothing. At least there was a distorted logic in knowing that the killing pain of a broken heart meant you were alive.

Beth had never felt more alive than she did at this moment. She had dark circles under her eyes from lack of sleep. And her eyes were swollen from crying. Her muscles were stiff and ached miserably. Her spirit was in agony, and her mind was stuck in replay. "Time apart . . . not your daughter . . . evaluate our relationship . . . never forgive myself . . . lousy example . . . an even greater mistake . . . I should never have listened to you . . ." her brain repeated continuously, the words bouncing painfully against her temples.

Jack hadn't come right out and told her they wouldn't be together anymore, but he would. Beth knew he would. She was a pro. She'd had men leave her before. And for far less cause than interfering with their daughter's welfare and refusing to marry them. Jack had valid reasons. He was angry because she wasn't ready to marry him. Her reluctance had led him into a relationship that embarrassed him because he had to sneak around. He felt shame and remorse because he felt he'd set a bad example for his daughter. He'd been forced to tell her, "Do as I say, not as I do." He'd lowered himself in his child's eyes—all because of Beth. Jack's only recourse was to leave her and try to right the wrong their relationship had caused in his daughter's life.

She understood this, but it didn't relieve any of the pain. At first she'd been angry, expecting more from Jack than to simply desert her at the first sign of trouble. But the more she thought about it, the more she realized that he didn't have much of a choice. If he gave in to Beth's fear, there was no telling how long their affair would go on. By terminating their relationship, he was giving in to her fears by proving them correct. Either way, her fear won out. But at least the latter solution gave him back his self-respect.

And Beth? Well, she'd given in to her fear a long time ago, hadn't she? She'd let it rule her life and keep Jack at a respectable distance, hadn't she?

She'd half expected him to leave her all along, hadn't she? And now she'd have to live with the truth. It wasn't Jack who was weak and unable to make a commitment. It was Beth. If she hadn't listened to her doubts, if she'd been able to believe that Jack was sincere . . .

She heard the front door open and close. She looked across the kitchen table to find Scotty gone. How long had she been sitting there in her bathrobe feeling sorry for herself? The thought was jolting. She felt disoriented and confused.

Immediately, she stood to go in search of Scott. Lord only knew what he'd been up to while she was semi-comatose.

"Beth?" she heard Jack call out as she pushed through the kitchen door into the small dining room. She walked into the entryway and saw Jack holding Scott. The boy removed Jack's cap and placed it on his head.

"I was getting worried," he said, visibly relieved when he saw her. "I've been out there knocking for ten minutes. Scotty let me in."

His words were short and clipped but laced with strain rather than with anger. He looked strained as well. He hadn't shaved. He was wearing the same clothes he'd had on the day before. His hair had been combed haphazardly, and he looked as if he hadn't slept in days.

"Jeez. You look horrible," he said, looking her over stem to stern, his brow creased with worry, his eyes full of concern. "Are you all right? Did Chelsea come here?"

"I'm fine," she lied, now seeing the agitation in his stance. His gaze moved restlessly from point to point as he shifted his weight. He was as antsy as a turkey on Thanksgiving Day.

"What's wrong, Jack. Why would Chelsea come here?"

Jack sighed heavily. "She's not here, then. I thought for sure she would be." He set Scott down on the floor and ran a hand distractedly through his hair. "You have no idea of the night I've had, Beth. Do you know your phone's off the hook?"

"I didn't feel like talking to my mother last night," she told him, assuming he'd understand why.

"I've been calling you all night. I made such a mess of everything. And then when I discovered she'd gone, I thought she was here and didn't want to talk to me. When you didn't call this morning to let me know she was all right, I called. But the line was still busy, so I came over." He rattled off his story as if she knew what he was talking about. Beth's own muddled mind was beginning to whirl. She felt as if she were blacking out and coming to in the middle of different conversations.

"Jack. I don't understand. You'll have to start at the beginning. Would you like some coffee?" It didn't matter whether he wanted coffee or not. *She* needed some to clear her head.

Jack followed her into the kitchen. She got out another mug and retrieved hers from the table.

"You're almost out of milk," he said with his head in the refrigerator.

"I know, Jack. Now tell me about Chelsea," she said curtly. He was acting as though he belonged in her kitchen. He'd been surprised by her appearance. He seemed to think it was the most natural thing in the world to come to her with his problems after they'd fought the day before and put their whole relationship on hold.

It wasn't that she minded exactly. She wanted to hear about Chelsea and help if she could. But she wished the man would make up his mind. Was she still involved in his life, or was she supposed to butt out?

He was quiet for a moment, gathering his thoughts. Scotty wandered in with a toy truck in one hand and a bulldozer in the other. He situated himself at Jack's feet and began to play.

Beth set Jack's coffee cup down on the table. He glanced up, and her heart went out to him automatically. He looked so forlorn.

"Remember when I left here yesterday?" he asked, eager to share his tale.

"Vividly."

"Well, I thought I had myself under control by the time I got home. I went in the house. I saw her, and then . . . I just sort of lost my mind. I wasn't really mad at her. In fact, I wanted to hold her, the way I used to when she was a baby. But I was so scared and so . . . oh, I don't know, just sick inside, you know? Anyway, I wasn't exactly tactful or patient with her. I came right out and asked her what she'd been doing at the clinic."

"What did she say?"

"Nothin'." He gave Beth an exasperated grimace. "She said she wasn't doing anything there. And *that's* when I got mad." She could tell by the sound of his voice that he hadn't been pleased with his reaction. He stepped over Scotty and began to pace around the room as he spoke. "But I was still trying to give her the benefit of the doubt. So I went down the list of possibilities you gave me. Was she hurt? No. Was

Boodle hurt? No. Was she working on a paper for school? Had she gone there for some information? 'Not exactly,' she said, 'Well, what *exactly* were you doing there,' I asked. Know what she said?"

Beth shook her head.

"She said she couldn't tell me."

"Why not?"

"She'd made a promise."

"To whom?"

"If I knew that, I'd have asked *them* what Chelsea was doing at the clinic," he declared testily, then instantly regretted his remark. "I'm sorry." He sat down beside her and picked up her right hand. He turned it over and studied it.

It occurred to her to pull away from him, but her hand felt as though it was home in his. It belonged there, and she was comfortably content to let it stay. She watched Scotty move his construction site around to the end of the table and once again begin to play between Jack's feet. Both she and Scotty were going to find it very hard to give Jack up.

"Is that when she left?" she asked him gently, wanting to help him deal with his anguish.

"No. We had a few more words after that." He was silent, as if recalling those words. Beth got the distinct impression that he wished they'd never been spoken. "I asked her if she was pregnant," he admitted in a low, soft voice. He reached out and smoothed Scotty's blond curls as if he needed to touch something innocent and good.

"Jack. You had to ask. You had to know. You had to."

He nodded his agreement. "But you should have seen the look on her face. She looked as if I'd slapped her. And then . . . then she looked disappointed. In me. She made me feel two inches tall."

"What did she say?"

"Well, she didn't say anything at first." He sighed, disheartened. "So I had to ask her again."

Beth could tell it was the toughest question he'd ever asked. He was so quiet for so long, she thought he might not finish the story. When he did speak his voice was weak with regret.

"She said no, she wasn't pregnant, and then she went to her room. I knocked on her door hours later, and she said she didn't really want to talk to me. I wanted to tell her I was sorry, but then I thought maybe we'd both be calmer in the morning, so I waited. I don't know how she got out of the house or how she got her car started without my hearing her, but when I passed her door on my way to bed, it was open and she was gone."

"She didn't go far, Jack. She loves you and she knows you too well. She knows you were only doing what you thought you had to do. She'll cool off and call."

"I hope so. I called my mom last night, thinking she might have gone there. Then I called and got Boodle out of bed. He's been calling me every five minutes since. When I called here and the line was busy, I thought maybe she was here and that she'd asked you to take the phone off the hook so I couldn't get through. I thought you'd call me later and let me know she was here, but . . . that was wishful thinking." He tried to smile reassuringly at her, but he didn't quite succeed.

"She'll call," Beth said confidently, feeling it in her heart. "I promise."

They sat for a long time watching Scotty play,

waiting to hear from Chelsea. They were both concerned. They both believed in Chelsea's good sense and knew she'd call. Silently, they shared their worries and supported each other. Beth felt as she never had before. She couldn't describe the feeling or put it into words. But in a way, in the most meaningful way, it felt as if they were already a family. The four of them shared a special bond of love and caring that seemed to grow even stronger in the face of adversity.

Her reverie was broken when Jack got up to refill their coffee cups. What would happen to this bond, this special family feeling when Chelsea came back and Jack left—for good. Having decided that their affair wasn't something he wanted his daughter to emulate, Jack was still going to leave her eventually.

"Shouldn't you be at home near the phone in case she calls?" she asked, suddenly feeling used and hurt. If he was going to leave he should do it quickly, the way her father and Cal had. Dragging it out would only make it worse.

"Mom came over early this morning to see if Chelsea was back. She said she'd stay by the phone until I called." He set the mug on the table and started moving toward the door that led to the living room. Scotty ran out of the room ahead of him. "I'll call and tell her to hang around a little longer."

"Why?"

Jack turned to face her. He looked confused and then uncertain. "Well, if it's all the same to you, I thought I'd stay here with you until we heard from her. I'll put Scotty's bed together while we wait."

"I already did. Last night."

"You didn't have to. I told you I'd do it."

Beth shrugged and kept her eyes trained on her

coffee. "I couldn't sleep, and I didn't have anything else to do. Scotty fell asleep in my bed last night, so . . . I just did it."

Jack seemed to sense that putting the bed together wasn't all she'd done during the night. When she looked up, he was leaning against the wall, watching her closely. "Anything else happen last night?" he asked, his tone guarded.

She shook her head. He didn't need to know that she had mourned and buried their love during the night. Why should she make it easy for him to leave?

"Would you rather I didn't stay today?" he asked.

"No. Yes. It's . . . up to you."

"Well, if it's up to me, then I'll stay. I need to be with you right now."

He stated his desire so simply and so sincerely that something snapped inside Beth. He didn't feel the slightest compunction in revealing his own needs, but what about hers? Who took care of her needs? Was she always supposed to stand idly by and let the men in her life dictate how much satisfaction she was allowed, how much pleasure, how much security and contentment? When would it be her turn to say, "I need you to stay with me," and have someone else listen?

All the times she'd held her tongue and accepted her fate at the hands of others flashed through her mind like a slide show. All the anger she'd felt, all the pain she'd had to bear and all the times she'd felt unworthy of being loved bubbled up inside her. From out of nowhere came a fury so strong, she felt like chewing the heads off nails.

"Well, great, Jack. You stay, then," she said irately standing up with so much force she knocked her chair over backward. "Our house is your house for as long as you need it. All I ask is that you close the door when you leave."

Jack's eyes narrowed and took on a keen, astute gleam as they watched her pick up Scott's breakfast dish and toss it into the sink. She stomped back to the table with a dishcloth, took a few swipes at the surface, and then threw the cloth at the faucet. He didn't speak until she looked ready to run from the room—and him.

"Who said I was leaving?" he asked, showing an uncanny ability to pick key words out of angry babble.

"No one had to say it. No one ever has to say it, it just happens. Suddenly one day everything turns sour, and then it's over. It doesn't matter if you want it to be over or not. It just disappears, and then there's nothing left," she ranted, trembling inside and out. Her eyes were stinging with tears, but she refused to let them fall.

"What the hell are you talking about? What's sour and what the hell is over?" Jack had pushed away from the wall and was standing rigidly, alert, ready to do combat with whatever came his way.

"Oh, Jack. Please don't pretend you don't know what I'm talking about. You don't need to let me down easy or try to spare my feelings. We both know what's happening, and I'd just as soon get it over with right now."

"Beth. Honey. I'm not pretending. Nothing you're saying makes sense to me, except for the fact that I don't like what I'm hearing. Start at the beginning. I'm totally lost," he said. He took several steps toward her, trying to close the physical distance between them. It was the emotional distance that made Beth back away from him.

"All right, Jack, let's say I did some evaluating and

rethinking of our relationship last night. Did you? Or did you already have your mind made up about us before you left the house yesterday? Because if it'll make it any easier for you, I'll tell you that I came to the same conclusion you did. Now you can leave with a clear conscience. I understand perfectly and—"

"Beth! Stop this. I don't know what the hell I said yesterday to get you going like this, but I'll tell you right now, you've got it all wrong." He paused to let his words sink in, and then added in a clear, level voice, "Except for one thing."

Beth gave him plenty of time to continue, but it soon became apparent that his silence was a dare for her to ask, "What?"

"I did have my mind made up about us before yesterday. Long before yesterday. The second time I saw you I knew for sure that I'd end up spending the rest of my life with you." He had clasped her by the shoulders before she saw him move. His fingers dug into her flesh, gripping her painfully. He bent his knees to be on a level with her eyes and looked directly into them when he spoke. "Nothing about that has changed since then. And it certainly hasn't changed since yesterday."

Now Beth was confused. "But you were so angry with me. Even before we ran into Chelsea. And then you were angrier because you'd set a bad example for her, and you were ashamed of having to sneak around to see me."

Jack tilted his head back and closed his eyes as if trying to gain control of himself. His touch on her upper arms was bruising, but she didn't think he realized it. He released a breath that seemed to come from the very depths of his soul, and then at last he looked down into her face.

For a long moment he studied her with a blend of emotions in his eyes that was both gentle and determined. Even his voice, when he spoke, was loaded with resolve. "I was angry. I was very angry. I get that way when I try everything I can think of to get what I want and fail." He used his index finger to lift her chin when her gaze fell away. "You, Beth Simms, are a very frustrating woman. I've done everything but stand on my head to get you to trust me. Hell, I'd do that, too, if I thought it would work. As for the example I set for my daughter, well, most of that was the original anger speaking, I'm afraid," he said, regretful. His palm caressed the side of her face as he traced her lips tenderly with his thumb. "Chelsea knows I don't sleep around with every pretty woman who comes through town. And she knows that what I feel for you is true and deep, because we've talked about it. If she does take my example, if she shows her love only to those she truly cares about, then I wouldn't have too much to complain about, would I?"

Beth shook her head. This wasn't the way she'd pictured their last moments together. His touch was draining away all the resentment and anger that had made her thoughts seem so valid. Where had she gone wrong?

"But I've shamed you. I make you sneak around to see me, and you hate it." She pointed this out, knowing that a man would resent a woman who made him look bad.

"You're damned right, I hate it. I've told you that before. I love you, and I want the whole world to know. I want you to marry me. I want you and everyone else to know what I know, that we belong together." He laughed as another thought occurred to him. "And I'm not exactly fooling anyone by going home at one in the morning either. The whole damned county knows we sleep together. The only real shame I feel is in not being able to find whatever it is you need to make you believe in me."

Frantically, Beth began digging up the grave she'd buried her love in the night before. What had she done? It was still alive and well, and she'd thrown it into a pit, covering it with a ton of old emotional debris.

"I'm not going to leave you, Beth," he continued to say. "Not now, not ever. I've never in my life loved anyone the way I do you. And if you think that when someone gets mad they're automatically going to leave, you're dead wrong. People in love fight. They get hurt and disappointed. They argue and disagree. But underneath it all they still love each other and they find ways to compromise." He grinned. "And then they get to make up."

In the nick of time Beth found her salvation. She'd spent most of her life looking for it, and there it was, in the grave with her great love for Jack. It was about to gasp its last breath, when she pressed it to her heart. She breathed life back into the belief that she was truly lovable, that Jack could love her no matter what. She revived an undespairing hope for a future of happiness and gratification. She reclaimed the trust she'd known as a child and placed it in her love for Jack.

"Jack." It wasn't much of a reply, especially after what she'd just discovered, but it was all she could get out around the thickness in her throat. Suddenly she was overflowing with thoughts and feelings and emotions she'd never known existed. She wanted to share them all with Jack, but she didn't know where to start.

Jack already knew. She could see it in his eyes. He knew something had changed. His smile was sweet and triumphant at once. He lowered his head and covered her mouth with his. His kiss was a deep search for all her new awareness, and she hid nothing from him.

He leaned back against the countertop for balance and pulled her close, pressing her small body into the contours of his large, hard frame. Beth tried to get even closer. There was nothing between them anymore, nothing to prevent a merging of their bodies, hearts, and souls. No tiny, invisible barrier to keep them apart.

"Say it," Jack murmured against her lips, his hands moving restlessly over her body. One big hand covered her breast while the other held her tight against his desire. "Say it for me, Beth."

"I love you," she said in a ragged voice. "I love you with all my heart," she said again, closing her eyes, focusing only on the pleasure and excitement of Jack's kisses as they crept slowly down her neck. Her robe slipped over her shoulder and her knees grew weak, while Jack very purposefully incited her body to riot with desire.

"Yak! Go ouside!" Scotty's voice rang through the room like a field marshal's command.

"I hate kids," Jack said with a growl, lifting his head from her breast and looking over her shoulder at Scott. "Let's not have too many more. Seven, eight tops."

"Tops," she agreed, grinning. "But let's make sure they all have better timing than this one."

"Well, maybe it's just as well we stopped now while we still could. Chelsea has a similar knack for interrupting things, and I'll need a clear head to talk to her when she calls."

"Yak. Go ouside now," Scott said again, more demanding this time as he pulled on Jack's leg.

Jack took the time to slowly, regretfully, close the front of Beth's robe. He took her face in his hands and kissed her sweetly. "Don't ever doubt my love again, Beth. If you have a question or you're worried about something I've said, talk to me. The only conclusion I want you to come to on your own about us is that I love you very much."

Beth smiled her agreement and her happiness. "I love you too," she said.

"Gets easier to say every time, doesn't it?" he said, teasing her, his eyes twinkling merrily as he gave his hand to Scott, allowing himself to be led away.

"Jack?" Beth called after him as something else occurred to her. He struggled to stop Scott at the kitchen door."If you weren't planning to leave me, what kind of evaluating and rethinking about our relationship were we supposed to be doing?"

"That wasn't a we as in you and me thinking separately. That was a we as in *you* giving some serious thought to changing the way you were thinking, and *me* helping you do it," he said. "I had my mind made up a long time ago about the way this would turn out. You were the one holding everything up."

That made sense to her. Jack had always known exactly what he wanted and what he had to do to get it. He knew who he was and where he was going. A chill shivered up Beth's back as she realized that for the first time in her life, she knew herself almost as well. There were certain powers and privileges a person who was truly loved and in love had that she hadn't tried or tested yet, but the confidence to do so was there inside her.

"Whoa, Scott. You can't go outside in your jammies. Let's go upstairs and get dressed first. Okay, pal?" Jack's low, deep voice comforted her. In every fiber of her being she knew that she would listen for that voice until the day she died. She would seek it out and listen to it. It would soothe her, excite her, and advise her. It might anger her and hurt her feelings, but it would be there always to give meaning and purpose to the familiar words, I love you.

The morning seemed unusually long as Beth and Jack tried to carry on as normally as possible while they waited for Chelsea to call or make an appearance. Still, under the tension and concern was something very new and stabilizing that helped them pass the time. A touch from Jack, a smile from Beth, they lent each other strength and tolerance.

Beth was cleaning up the dishes from lunch, a peculiar meal of canned fruit and leftovers, as there wasn't much else in the house. Jack was in Scott's room tightening the bolts on the new bed, which had a tendency to sway and squeak when the little boy bounced on it, much to Jack's pleasure and Beth's dismay. These acts were time fillers. Indeed, the whole house seemed tuned in, listening for the phone to ring.

Beth all but jumped out of her skin when the call finally came. Something upstairs clattered to the floor, and she heard Jack's thundering steps before she could get to the phone to answer it.

"Chelsea, honey, where are you?" she asked, knowing the girl's voice instantly. "Your dad and I have been worried sick about you."

"I know and I'm sorry," she said. "But I just couldn't face Dad this morning. He'd have asked me again about the clinic, and I would have had to lie to him again. So I left."

"Where are you now?"

"At home. I drove by your house and saw his car there, so I came here. Gramma said he was waiting for me to call."

"He is. He's very worried about you."

"I know, but . . . well, I was hoping I could talk to you first. I . . . I thought maybe you could help me explain it to him." She sounded so bewildered and in need, Beth was hard put to refuse her, even though she knew it was Jack's dilemma to solve.

"Explain what?" she asked, turning to Jack, who had come to her side, eager to speak to his daughter. She put a reassuring hand on his chest and begged him with her eyes to be patient and to trust *her* this time.

"What I was doing at the clinic yesterday. Boodle didn't tell him, did he? Because he promised he wouldn't."

"No, Boodle didn't tell. But he's been as worried about you as we have."

"I already called him."

"Good," Beth said, trying to stay objective, eager for Chelsea to get to the point. "Now tell me what happened yesterday."

"Well . . ." She was obviously trying to choose her words carefully. "When Dad got home yesterday, he was really mad about seeing me at the clinic. He asked me what I was doing there, but I couldn't tell him because I'd promised a friend that I wouldn't."

"You mean you went there to get something for a friend and promised this friend you wouldn't tell anyone about it."

"Right." She seemed pleased that Beth was so intuitive. "And then he got even madder and asked me if I was pregnant."

"I know, Chelsea. And he feels awful about it, but he was very worried. I think you can understand why."

"Yeah, I do," she said with a little laugh. "When I turned thirteen we had this really long talk. About him and my mom, you know? He used to say he wished I had buck teeth and wore glasses, so he wouldn't have to worry so much."

"He just loves you, you know."

"Yeah. I know. The thing is, he was right yesterday. About why I was at the clinic."

"What?" Beth's heart skipped a beat and her mind went blank.

"Oh, not me. My friend. She's pregnant, and she's real scared. She asked me to go to the clinic and get some stuff for her to read before she makes an appointment. Once she does that, her folks are bound to find out. She asked me to go so she could put off telling them a little longer and have her mind made up about what she wanted to do."

"Oh," Beth said, her voice squeaking on her sigh of relief. "But, Chelsea, why didn't you just tell your father all of this. He would have understood."

"Are you kidding? My dad? Mr. Superstraight? He'd have asked me who the friend was. And if I'd told him, he'd have told her parents, because he thinks parents need to know this kind of stuff."

"Well, they do. They need to know so they can help."

"She'll tell them. She's just not ready to yet."

"I see. Well, will you tell her for me that the sooner she tells them, the more help they can give her."

"I did. But her folks aren't exactly like you and my dad. They'd never understand. Which is why I couldn't take the chance of having Dad talking to them before she was ready for them to know. And if he'd asked me too much, I'm sure I would have started to look guilty, and then he'd have really been after me. I left so I wouldn't have to talk to him, and he wouldn't have to get mad at me for not telling the truth." Chelsea made her actions sound logical, as if she'd had no alternative. Knowing Chelsea, Beth could understand her loyalty to her friend and her reluctance to lie to her father. Removing herself was probably the best solution she could come up with at the time.

"Well, that makes sense to me. But you've worried your dad sick. And if you really want my opinion, I think if you explained all of this to him, he'd understand. I think you'll find he's a little more reasonable—"

"I am totally reasonable," Jack muttered in a low voice beside her. "At all times."

"—and objective when he's not dealing with the people he loves the most. He'd also be a good person for your friend to come to for some advice if she needs it," Beth told her, rolling her eyes heavenward for Jack's benefit. From what he'd heard of the conversation, he had apparently gotten the general story line and surmised that Chelsea was safe. He was obviously feeling much better.

"You think so?" Chelsea didn't sound too convinced.

"Yes, I do. Don't you?"

"Maybe."

"He's waiting to talk to you."

She heard the girl breathe in and out heavily, preparing for the worst. "Okay."

Beth handed the phone to Jack, and they smiled at each other in that secret way parents had when they'd weathered yet another storm in their child's life. He kissed her quickly, softly, on the lips and whispered, "Thanks," before placing the receiver to his ear.

"Chelsea? I'm sorry about yesterday."

Beth scooped up Scotty and walked back into the kitchen with him to give father and daughter some privacy. The little boy wiggled and protested loudly until she set him down on the floor again. Also against his wishes she planted a kiss on the top of his head. She had a feeling that in the years to come she'd be very glad to have Jack around to be Scotty's father.

In fact, she had a feeling there were going to be many things she liked about having Jack around.

Twelve

Now, where have I heard this story before?

The hotel manager's wife cast a discrediting eye in Jack's direction.

"I swear, Mrs. White," he said, trying to look totally innocent. "She's been as grumpy and mean as an old grizzly bear right from the start. Nothing pleases her. Not that I blame her, mind you. She's as big as Mount Casey. Just look at her," he said, motioning at an unsuspecting Beth, who was sitting in the car parked just outside the hotel's office door.

"Well, I can't tell if she's pregnant or not, but she doesn't look mean or grumpy to me, Mr. Reardan," the woman said kindly.

Jack's expression was pained. "Take my word for it, appearances can be very deceptive. You have no idea what I'll have to live through if I can't manage to persuade you to give us the same room we had last time we were here. You see, she makes me remember all these weird little anniversaries of things we did while we were dating. Like the first time we spoke, the first time we kissed, the first time we . . . well, the list goes on and on, but she was so happy the last time we were here, and it turned out so well with your help, well—" His expression was so ingratiating. "I thought I'd surprise her by remembering this one on my own. Our first snow-in, so to speak."

"Mr. Reardan, I have the distinct impression that you're pulling my leg, but I can't bring myself to come right out and call you a liar. I rather fancy a romantic gentleman myself. But the fact remains that the room you want is already occupied. The best I can do is give you the one adjoining it."

"And you don't think, if we explained the circumstances to these people, that they might give up the room?"

"I'm positive."

Jack was crestfallen. "I guess the room next door will have to do, then," he said with a sigh of defeat. "I brought my own candles, but I'll need an excuse to be out of the room to get them before my wife takes her bath. Do you think you could call the room and ask me to come back down to the office for some reason or other? Say about eight-thirty or so?"

"I'd be glad to, Mr. Reardan. Did you remember the wine too?"

Jack grinned. "Yep."

Billions and billions of stars twinkled down on them from light-years away. The snow crunched under their feet, and the wind blew cold against their unprotected cheeks. Their breath made clouds and floated skyward as it escaped with their laughter.

"That's not fair, Jack. I can't even reach the top of your coat without a ladder," Beth protested, wiggling convulsively to dislodge the snow he'd stuck down her back.

"Everything is fair in a snowball fight," he said, laughing mercilessly at her gyrations. "Ask Scott, he'll tell you."

"Oh, sure. And who taught him all about it?"

With his hands on his hips and a smug, superior expression on his face, he bent forward and said, "His dad did."

"That figures. That guy hasn't played fair since the day I met him," she said, scooping a handful of snow off the hood of the car in the hotel parking lot.

He was proud to be Scott's father and that alone was another of the many special reasons she'd found for loving Jack. She'd asked him once if it ever bothered him that he wasn't Scott's biological father, and he'd said, "Hell, no. A smart kid like that? He knew who I was the minute he saw me." Of course, after that she'd never told him that Scott had called Jim McKenzie Daddy first.

Jack had done some scouting and found a cozy little restaurant three blocks from the hotel. What had started, for Beth, as a Sunday afternoon drive had been turned into another anniversary surprise. She had to pretend her amazement when they pulled up in front of the hotel they'd stayed at with Chelsea and her friends the year before. She knew full well the ride would end there. Jack had been doing such things all year. He'd even gone so far as to make her drink champagne on the roof one afternoon.

But once the initial shock wore off, she wasn't at

all amazed to see him pull a suitcase out of the trunk or have him lead her to the same room she'd had that night. He had been disappointed that they couldn't get *their* room, but Beth wasn't at all.

She could hardly remember the woman who had spent that first night in the hotel room with Jack. That suspicious, insecure woman was a pitiful part of her past. The woman spending the evening with Jack on this particular night was secure, content, and a little overloved, if that were possible. Jack was an attentive husband, a demonstrative lover, and a caring companion. He had a talent for making her feel special. He taught her how to live in the present and remember only as far back as the day they met.

Their dinner had been romantic and filled with the promise of the night to come. They walked back to the hotel hand in hand, hardly aware of the crisp, cold air that blew in the opposite direction. Jack was telling her about the long song and dance he'd had to give the proprietor's wife in order to get the room closest to the one they'd shared the first night. And that's when Beth tried to punish him with the first snowball for lying so horribly.

Jack had seen her gathering snow for her next assault and hadn't been about to be caught unprepared. While he'd bent over for more ammo, Beth had made two snowballs—one to throw and one to keep as a spare. He'd pelted her twice, and she'd hit him once then had waited for him to bend over again.

"Jack," she said sweetly. "You really shouldn't be throwing snowballs at me."

"Oh, yeah? Why not?" he asked, hardly glancing up from his task.

"Well, what would Mrs. White say if she saw you throwing snowballs at the mother of your next child."

"That's very good, Beth. But I really don't think she believed me any more this time than she did the last time we were here. She probably thinks I'm a compulsive liar, so she won't be surprised to see that you aren't pregnant." He turned and tossed a snowball menacingly from one hand to the other. "But that was a good try, honey. Now be prepared for the fight of your life."

"But what if I could prove to Mrs. White that you weren't lying. Then how would you feel?"

Jack's face grew deadly serious. His eyes narrowed to study her intently, to see if this was another one of her tricks to get out of a losing battle. She saw the hope and the desire to believe her that came to his eyes with his excitement. His voice was hardly more than a whisper when he finally spoke.

"Can you prove it?" he asked, his body taut with anticipation.

Beth just grinned and wiggled her brows in a Jacklike fashion. But it was all the answer he needed. His whoop rose up in the vacant parking lot and echoed off the hotel walls before he grabbed her up in his arms and swung her around and around in circles.

That he was so ecstatic only increased the warm glow of happiness and fulfillment that Beth had been carrying around inside her for the past three days. If dreams really did come true—and she was now a firm believer that they did—she was living in hers.

Jack danced her back to their room and was giggling to himself in the bathroom when the phone rang.

"Oh, dear," Beth said, anxious. "I hope that's not your mother calling to tell us Scotty's stuck another marble up his nose."

"Bite your tongue," Jack told her, picking up the phone. He was acting very businesslike to whomever was on the other end, and Beth sighed with relief. "That was the desk. They want me to go down and move the car so the snowplow can get through. Go ahead and take your bath if you want. I'll be right back."

"Do you think you could pick up something to drink while you're out?"

"No problem."

Jack was excited to get back, but he wanted to give Beth plenty of time to get in the tub. When she came out, she'd find the room filled with candles, as it had been before. He loved doing things like this for her. She was always so pleased, so touched.

He was careful to be quiet when he let himself into the room again. But when he turned around, a chill colder than the winter winds outside passed through him. The room was empty. The bathroom light was off, the bed was still made, and Beth was nowhere to be seen.

"Beth?" he called out automatically, even though he knew she wasn't there.

He heard a rustling to his right and saw that the door to the next room was ajar. "Beth?" he called again, pulling the door open wide and stepping through it.

Carrying a shopping bag full of candles and a bottle of wine in his arms, he stood dumbfounded in the doorway. There already were lit candles all around the room, and his beautiful wife lay in the bed, the sheet barely covering her breasts. She was looking very cocky and clever as she held a glass of wine out to him.

"Some of us know how to call ahead and make reservations," she said, teasing him. "Some of us even know how to get Mrs. White to cooperate with candles and phone calls. But then, not all of us have taken lessons from the master romantic."

Jack smirked. "That's me, right?"

She just smiled at his conceit. Without taking his eyes off his wife, he dropped his shopping bag in a nearby chair and removed his coat. It occurred to him that if pregnancy was going to make her glow, he'd have to get sunglasses. Beth always glowed. She wore her happiness on her face like a skin cream that made her more beautiful every day.

His bulky knit ski sweater came off next. He stepped around the bed and sat down beside her, leaning over to untie and remove his shoes. When he was ready, he planted his hands on either side of her pelvis and looked into the eyes that had never been able to lie to him.

"Tell me, Mrs. Reardan, are you happy about this pregnancy?" he asked, knowing the answer but wanting to be absolutely sure.

"I'm thrilled, Mr. Reardan," she said without hesitation.

"And have I told you today how very much I love you?"

"Well, not in so many words. But then, I like it better when you show me anyway. And I've seen it all day long."

"And would you like to see it all night long as well?"

She placed the palm of her hand to his cheek, adoring the strength and warmth of his face. "More than anything," she said.

Their loving was confirmation of all they aspired to in life. Every hope, every dream, every need, every care, was met in a communion so perfect and fulfilling, no familiar words could describe it.

THE EDITOR'S CORNER

This month we're inaugurating a special and permanent feature that is dear to our hearts. From now on we'll spotlight one Fan of the Month at the end of the Editor's Corner. Through the years we've enjoyed and profited from your praise, your criticisms, your analyses. So have our authors. We want to share the joy of getting to know a devoted romance reader with all of you other devoted romance readers—thus, this feature. We hope you'll enjoy getting to know our first Fan of the Month, Pat Diehl.

Our space is limited this month due to the addition of our new feature, so we can give you only a few tasty tidbits about each upcoming book.

Leading off is Kay Hooper with LOVESWEPT #360, **THE GLASS SHOE,** the second in her *Once Upon a Time* series. This modern Cinderella story tells the tale of beautiful heiress Amanda Wilderman and dashing entrepreneur Ryder Foxx, who meet at a masquerade ball. Their magical romance will enchant you, and the fantasy never ends—not even when the clock strikes midnight!

Gail Douglas is back with *The Dreamweavers*: **GAMBLING LADY,** LOVESWEPT #361, also the second in a series. Captaining her Mississippi riverboat keeps Stefanie Sinclair busy, but memories of her whirlwind marriage to Cajun rogue T.J. Carriere haunt her. T.J. never understood what drove them apart after only six months, but he vows to win his wife back. Stefanie doesn't stand a chance of resisting T.J.—and neither will you!

LOVESWEPT #362, **BACK TO THE BEDROOM** by Janet Evanovich, will have you in stitches! For months David Dodd wanted to meet the mysterious woman who was always draped in a black cloak and carrying a large, odd case—and he finally gets the chance when a helicopter drops a chunk of metal through his lovely neighbor's roof and he rushes to her rescue. Katherine Finn falls head over heels for David, but as a dedicated concert musician, she can't fathom the man who seems to be drifting through life. This wonderful story is sure to strike a chord with you!

Author Fran Baker returns with another memorable romance, **KING OF THE MOUNTAIN,** LOVESWEPT #363. Fran deals with a serious subject in **KING OF THE MOUNTAIN,** and she handles it beautifully. Heroine Kitty

(continued)

Reardon carries deep emotional scars from a marriage to a man who abused her, and hero Ben Cooper wants to offer her sanctuary in his arms. But Kitty is afraid to reach out to him, to let him heal her soul. This tenderly written love story is one you won't soon forget.

Iris Johansen needs no introduction, and the title of her next LOVESWEPT, #364, **WICKED JAKE DARCY,** speaks for itself. But we're going to tantalize you anyway! Mary Harland thinks she's too innocent to enchant the notorious rake Jake Darcy, but she's literally swept off her feet by the man who is temptation in the flesh. Dangerous forces are at work, however, forcing Mary to betray Jake and begin a desperate quest. We bet your hearts are already beating in double-time in anticipation of this exciting story. Don't miss it!

From all your cards and letters, we know you all just love a bad-boy hero, and has Charlotte Hughes got one for you in **SCOUNDREL,** LOVESWEPT #365. Growing up in Peculiar, Mississippi, Blue Mitchum had been every mother's nightmare, and every daughter's fantasy. When Cassie Kennard returns to town as Cassandra D'Clair, former world-famous model, she never expects to encounter Blue Mitchum again—and certainly never guessed he'd be mayor of the town! Divorced, the mother of twin girls, Cassie wants to start a new life where she feels safe and at home, but Blue's kisses send her into a tailspin! These two people create enough heat to singe the pages. Maybe we should publish this book with a warning on its cover!

Enjoy next month's LOVESWEPTs and don't forget to keep in touch!

Sincerely,

Carolyn Nichols

Carolyn Nichols
Editor
LOVESWEPT
Bantam Books
666 Fifth Avenue
New York, NY 10103

LOVESWEPT IS PROUD
TO INTRODUCE OUR FIRST
FAN OF THE MONTH

Pat Diehl

I was speechless when Carolyn Nichols called to say she wanted me to be LOVESWEPT's first **FAN OF THE MONTH,** but I was also flattered and excited. I've read just about every LOVESWEPT ever published and have corresponded with Carolyn for many years. I own over 5,000 books, which fill two rooms in my house. LOVESWEPT books are "keepers," and I try to buy them all and even get them autographed. Sometimes I reread my favorites—I've read **LIGHTNING THAT LINGERS** by Sharon and Tom Curtis twenty-seven times! Some of my other favorite authors are Sandra Brown, Joan Elliott Pickart, Billie Green, and Mary Kay McComas, but I also enjoy reading the new authors' books.

Whenever I come across a book that particularly moves me, I buy a copy, wrap it in pretty gift paper, and give it to a senior citizen in my local hospital. I intend to will all my romance books to my granddaughter, who's now two years old. She likes to sit next to me and hold the books in her hands as if she were reading them. It's possible that there could be another **FAN OF THE MONTH** in the Diehl family in the future!